I'M NOT YOUR DIFFERENCE

FITZ SERIES BOOK FOUR

USA TODAY BESTSELLING AUTHOR

THERESA SEDERHOLT

I'm Not Your Difference
A Fitz Series Book 4

This book contains strong language, and violence. It is not intended for anyone under the age of 18.

Publisher: Theresa Sederholt©
Author: Theresa Sederholt
Cover designer: Sweet 15 Designs
Formatter: Stacey Blake, Champagne Book Design
Editor: Jacquelyn Ayres

Andy's story has been weighing heavy on my mind for a long time. Sadly, it's a reality for so many people. Not everyone fits into the same box. If that was the case, this world would be so boring. This book is dedicated to the people who combat ignorance with knowledge and show kindness and caring to everyone.

"People are people. I wish we lived in a world without labels. I really believe that's where the trouble begins." ~Fitz.

Stay Humble, be kind
As Always, Hugs.
Theresa Sederholt

I'M NOT YOUR DIFFERENCE

FITZ SERIES BOOK FOUR

Prologue

Stone

Looking in the mirror, I don't see the man with the chiseled Hollywood features. I don't see those cute dimples that everyone raves about. I see the broken little boy who was made to feel like a dirty little freak. At thirteen, I knew I was different. I couldn't understand why. My friends would talk about girls, and I felt nothing. My best friend Jimmy would steal his father's Penthouse magazine. Then he would pass it around as we took turns getting ourselves off. Everyone, that is, except me. I became a joke to them. The more I tried and couldn't, the more they would ridicule me. Finally, I went to my father, asking for help. Was I embarrassed? Hell yeah, but I was desperate to fit in. What I got was a whipping with his belt. He said he knew all too well what I was feeling. He fought the same feelings when he was my age. Every time I felt the urge, I would go to my father so he could beat it out of me.

As I grew older, I realized the beatings did nothing. All it did was to lead me down the path of despair. The despair I live with on a daily basis. My only mission now is to convince men like me that no one would want them, not like they are. These men are damaged goods, at best. I've helped them to rid themselves of the guilt they've felt all their lives. It wasn't always easy to manipulate their thoughts, but, in the end, I believe all they wanted was the same thing that I've always wanted: to fit in. I learned to take my time and convince them that the best thing they can do is kill the demon that lives inside of them. Ultimately, it's the only way. Of course, I was always there to help them along when they needed it. I've found the easiest way to find people like me is on dating websites. Damaged men like me are served up on a silver platter. This last one was hard. It took longer to convenience the good doctor Arman into believing that his mother was ashamed of him. I made him understand his god would forgive him. He had to put his mother first and end the shame he knew she was feeling.

Society today says it's acceptable to be whatever you want to be. So, that's what I'm doing—fitting in. Ridding the world of what was unacceptable in the past. Maybe if I can rid the world of them, then all these feelings that are buried deep inside of me will finally be gone. The beast inside of me will die along with them one man at a time.

Chapter One

Fitz

Life is good. No, scratch that—my life is fantastic. I've found a balance between work and my real life. So, when Andy, my best friend and brother-in-law, showed up for coffee just now visibly upset, I put everything aside to help him. I pour us each a cup and wait for him to start. He glances around as if he's trying to figure out how to begin. I decide to put him out of his misery. "We're alone, but you knew that already, so what's bothering you?" I ask. He looks me in the eye, but then quickly looks away. This can't be good.

"Stephen contacted me. He wants to meet up. I decided to go, and before you say anything, no one knows . . . and I *mean* no one."

I take a deep breath and slowly exhale, giving myself the time to calm down. What he is telling me is MJ, his sister and my wife, doesn't know. "Why?"

"He reached out to me. He said we had unfinished business."

"Do you?" As I try to remain calm on the outside, I can feel the blood coursing through my veins.

"I didn't think so, but then he said he wanted me, Fitz. He said he needed me."

I have a grip on my cup so tight, I think I might break it. In my mind, I'm counting to ten, reaffirming to myself that Andy is an adult and he knows what he's doing. "He wanted you! He needed you! Andy, he walked the fuck out on you. He didn't want you to have a life. He crushed your dreams. Stephen used all the difficulties of your Parkinson's like a weapon against you. Did you forget that and the fact that he didn't want Stella? Stella, Andy—your daughter—the one person who gives you purpose." I can't believe he would even consider giving him another chance. Another chance to hurt him, to hurt all of us. "I know that after your diagnosis, having a child was never in yours and Stephen's wheelhouse. However, when MJ became pregnant, it opened up a door that you thought you sealed up for good. Stephen was not willing to listen to what you needed. All he did was make it about your Parkinson's. I watched you, Andy, every day a bit more closed off to the world around you. Then Stella happened. Yes, it was terrible that the only parent she had ever known was murdered, but I believe God put her in our path. She needed a family and so did you. When she legally became your daughter, you changed. I've got to tell you, watching that change has been inspiring. Stella has changed all of us. She might be deaf, but she never lets that get in the way of loving her life. She's taught us all how to live a complete life, even if we are a little different. Bringing Stephen back into the picture would put all of that into jeopardy."

"Fitz, this is not like you. You're such a forgiving person. Did you ever think that maybe he realized he was wrong? Maybe he wants to make amends."

"This is not about me. And for the record, you can forgive someone, but that doesn't mean you let that person back into your inner circle. Jesus, Andy, what the hell are you thinking? Again, what about Stella? It's not just you anymore," I remind him. He gets up and pushes his chair in. "Where do you think you're going?" I fly out of my chair so fast, I knock it over.

"Apparently, we're done here. You know I always put Stella first, so don't you dare throw that in my face. Everyone comes to you for help and you're all in. I'm here, just needing my best friend to talk to. To help me understand what I'm feeling, and you freak out. I've never known you to be so close-minded, least of all with me."

He turns and heads toward the door and I'm right on his heels. Now I feel like shit. "Andy, wait. You're right." I reach out and grab his arm. "Come on, let's sit down and talk about it. I promise not to be too much of an ass."

He looks at his watch and takes another step toward the door. "Don't worry about it, Fitz. MJ should be back any minute with the kids, and I don't want her to know any of this."

Great, now I have to try to keep this from my wife, too. Before I can protest, all hell breaks loose. The kids are running up the stairs with the dogs at their heels. Livy comes in all out of breath while MJ is trying to corral everyone. Livy is two days over her due date and she's doing everything from Yoga to power walking to start labor. She begged Travis to drive her up and down the city streets with the worst potholes on his Harley, no less. He finally talked her out of that one. Yesterday, I asked her how she felt and she damn near ripped me a new one.

"Livy, would you like me to fix you something to eat?" I offer. She rolls her eyes and the smile she has quickly fades. She gets a look I've seen before. The same one MJ had right before she went into labor.

"Fitz, I'm having the worst back pains. I don't need food. What I need is for this kid to get out of me already." Then she cries, damn it. I can't handle tears.

"Where the hell is Travis?"

"I sent him to work before he made me shoot him."

"Okay, I know you're joking, but please don't shoot my friend. I enjoy having him around."

"He keeps staring at my belly like he's waiting for the baby to burst through any minute, like the scene from *Alien*."

I try not to laugh, but I can't help it. "He's nervous; it's only normal. I promise, once the baby gets here, he will lighten up."

Andy heads to the coffee bar and pours himself a cup. Yes, we have an actual coffee bar in our kitchen. Don't judge until you've walked in my shoes. When he turns around, MJ is blatantly staring at him. *Yeah, good luck trying to keep anything from that woman, buddy.* Before she can weasel it out of him, Livy grabs onto MJ's arm. Her jaw is tight and her eyes are wide. "I think my water broke, either that or I've taken up peeing in my pants," she announces calmly.

"Andy, call Travis and tell him it's time. Let him know we will pick him up along the way. Take care of the kids till we get back. MJ, run next door and get her bag while I help her down the steps." I begin barking orders without missing a beat. I bend down to lift her up when she digs her nails into my shoulder.

"I can walk, Fitz. Just give me your arm to hold on to."

We head toward the stairs when another contraction hits. She leans completely into me, and takes in deep, slow breaths. "I think it's safe to say those back pains you've been having were contractions." I want to scoop her up and race down the steps, but the death look I just got leads me to give her the chance to try walking again. When we finally get to the car, with MJ's help, I get her settled into the back seat just as Travis comes running out of the alley. The office is only two blocks away; I knew he couldn't wait for us. He climbs in the back and begins doing everything he learned in the Lamaze classes they took. MJ pulls out her phone and starts timing her contractions. She glances at me with her bottom lip between her teeth. I know this is not the time that my cock should take notice of how sexy my wife is. Some things are just out of my control, that is, until MJ turns her phone towards me, showing me that Livy's contractions are a minute apart. My oh shit, *this-can't-be-happening-to-me-in-my-car* mode kicks in.

"Hang on, Livy, I promise you your baby will be born in a hospital." I hit the gas and break all the rules while MJ gets 911 on the line.

"I want to push. How much further?" Livy shouts.

I tilt the rear-view mirror down so I can try to see what is going on back there. God bless Travis, he's trying his best to help her, but when he suggests massaging her, Livy's eyes close tight and she lets out a growling sound that scares even me. "Livy, do you still have the urge to push?" I ask, trying to distract her.

"Fitz, forget about the urge, this baby wants out. You better hurry!" she yells as she is trying to control her breathing.

All my years on the force, I never delivered a baby. However, I was present for the birth of both my kids and, honestly, that was enough for me. I barrel into the parking lot of the hospital. Thankfully, there is a team outside the emergency room entrance waiting for us.

While they quickly get her inside, I park the car and say a brief prayer that they will both be okay. I mean, I have a direct line to the big guy upstairs. When I head inside and find MJ texting someone with that look I know all too well on her face. It's the one where she wants to throttle someone. Thankfully, for once, it's not me.

"Hey, babe, what's the status on Livy?" Classic distraction move. She rolls her eyes and sticks her phone into her back pocket.

"Travis should be out soon. What the hell is going on with Andy?"

Before I can answer, Travis comes through the door with a smile from ear to ear. I'm silently screaming, *thank you, man, for saving my ass.*

"It's a girl! Eight pounds, four ounces. Everyone is okay."

We're all hugging and happy that everything turned out okay.

I'm hoping this is the distraction that will keep MJ from asking me anything more about Andy. I give Travis's shoulder a squeeze. "So, are you finally going to reveal her name? I mean, I can't believe you kept this a secret the whole time."

"Piper Ann. Thank God she looks like Livy. I'm going back in there. After they get settled, I'll come back out and get you." He goes running back to Livy and now it's just us. I take a deep breath and prepare myself for what I know is coming.

"Fitz, why don't you just tell me what's going on with Andy? In the end, you know you're going to anyway, so make this easy on both of us."

She has a point, but a promise is a promise, and I'm a man of my word. "I know very little because we got interrupted. Besides, whatever he told me was told in confidence."

"I don't want to see him hurt."

"Well, I don't either, but he's an adult, and he has to live his life as he sees fit. If he stumbles, then we'll be there to help him pick up the pieces. Now, I want to check on Livy and meet Piper." We get up and head off to see Livy and Piper. Mother and daughter are doing great. Piper has a lot of strawberry-blonde hair. Travis wasn't kidding when he said she looks like Livy.

While MJ and Livy are cooing over the baby, Travis pulls me to the side. "What's up?"

"Before I left the office, Father O'Neil called looking for you."

"That's odd; he never calls. Usually, he catches me after Sunday mass. Did he say what he needed?"

"No, he didn't. It was odd because if he needed help with something at the church, he would have asked me."

Travis is right, it's very odd. "I'll stop by the church after I drop MJ off at home. Now maybe I can hold my niece if I can pry her out of MJ's hands."

MJ passes her to me and as I look at her, I thank God for this beautiful gift. "Piper, you are so beautiful. Welcome to our family, sweet girl."

She starts to get fussy. I pass her back to Livy. "We are going to go now and let you rest. If you need anything, let me know." As MJ and I head out, I look back over my shoulder and smile at the three of them huddled together. A perfect family.

Chapter Two

When we get home, MJ goes upstairs. I know she's going to get into it with Andy. I need to stay out of this, so I decide to walk over to the church and see what Father O'Neil needed. This time of day it's quiet inside and it's here that I do my best thinking. After lighting a candle and saying a few thank you prayers, I head into the rectory in search of Father O'Neil. It doesn't take me long to find him in his outer office, attempting to fix a paper jam in the printer.

"Hi, Father, I'm here to put you out of your misery." He laughs and steps aside while I quickly clear up the problem. "This printer has seen better days, Father. You might want to look into getting a new one."

"That would be nice, but it's not in the budget for at least another year."

"I'll pray about it for you." We both laugh. "Travis said you needed to talk to me."

"Yes, but first things first. Did he make it home in time, and how is Olivia?"

"Yes, he did. We barely made it to the hospital. Piper Ann came into the world safe and sound. She's a cutie; looks just like Livy."

"Let's go into my office, where it's quiet."

His office is set up more like a living room. A desk with a chair in the corner is more like an afterthought. There is a television that still has knobs you turn by hand, two chairs, a coffee table, and a love seat. Everything was donated, so nothing matches but it's extremely comfortable. He goes to his desk to retrieve a file and when he hands it to me, I sit in one chair as he takes the one next to me. As I begin going through the file, I realize it's pretty thick. There are six obituary clippings. Then there is an autopsy report and some handwritten letters.

"Okay, so do you want to tell me what this is all about?" I look up and ask. He's hesitating, which is not like him. I have an idea. "Father, think of it as a confessional. What we say here is between you, me, and God."

"This is new for me, Fitz. I'm usually on the receiving end of things. Mrs. Blankenship is a parishioner here. Her son Arman was not a member of this parish. He lived in the lower east side of the city and he was gay. I'm only telling you this because it has to do with why I needed to see you. She came to me last week with this folder. About a month ago, Arman died. According to the medical examiner, he committed suicide. As you can see from the obituary clippings, there have been many suicides in the gay community. Mrs. Blankenship doesn't believe it was suicide. She is of the school of thought that suicide is equivalent to a mortal sin. She said Arman was a doctor and loved life. I've tried everything I could think of to help her through this. Nothing is working. The other night I read everything in that folder repeatedly and now . . . even I have doubts."

He gets up and pulls two water bottles from his mini fridge. He passes me one and sits back down. I spread the obits out and put them in chronological order. I pull out the handwritten letters and quickly scan them. They are all upbeat, except for the last one. That's a letter that was no doubt intended to be a goodbye note. "Did you speak to the police about this?"

"No, because, honestly, I'm not sure what to think. Did he take his own life or was his death made to look that way? Am I watching too many crime shows?—probably. Do you think you can investigate this? I might be able to scrape together some money to pay you for your time."

I quickly hold my hand up, stopping him from continuing. "You don't have to pay me. I'll look into this and see what I can find out. Is Mrs. Blankenship aware of the fact that you were coming to me with all of this?"

"Yes, I had to ask her if it was what she wanted. I can give you her contact information and, if you have questions, you can contact her directly." He passes me a piece of paper with her information on it.

"Can I keep all of this?" I wave my hand over the pile of papers on the table.

"Yes. Thank you, Fitz. I'll sleep better knowing that you are on this."

"I'm not promising anything other than I will look into it. It could just be coincidence." Even though I don't believe in coincidences, but I don't want to get his hopes up. Quickly, I gather everything and head out. I'm only a block away from the office. I'll head over there and take the time I need time to look over everything. If Hudson is available, I can even run it past her. She's a good sounding board. I think she's on a 4-12 shift this month, so I might catch her in time. When I get there, she is just heading out. "Hey, where are you heading to?"

"I'm going to see Livy and the baby and then to work. Do you need me for something?"

I want to keep her here with me, but I know she's been so excited about the baby. I don't want to take that away from her. "No, you don't have to worry. I'm going to look into something for a friend. I'm sure it's nothing, but if I need you, I'll call you."

She leaves, but not before warning me to stay out of trouble. Since I'm the only one here, I decide to set up shop in the conference room. I lay everything out and make a board with a chain of events. I start by reading the obits more closely. I remember seeing some of them, but, at the time, I was just flipping through the paper while having my morning coffee. Every one of the suicide victims was a man. I put their names into the internet and check any social media sites. The men are all around the same age. They all live in Brooklyn, but work in different boroughs. Every one of them is some sort of professional: doctors, lawyers, and accountants. Do they know each other? What's the connection? The only thing that they had in common is they were gay—big deal. People are people. I wish we lived in a world without labels. I really believe that's where the trouble begins, but I digress.

I pin them on the board and pull out the letters. Why write letters? Does anyone do that anymore? As I read them, I feel like I'm intruding. They are personal letters from a son to a mother. The last letter is the goodbye to his mom.

I'm sorry, Mom. Please know I never meant to embarrass you. I thought I it was okay to be who I am. Being gay was something that I wanted to believe was normal. Now I realize now I'm not right. It's eating away at me. I don't want you to be ashamed of me anymore. I love you, Mom.

Arman

Dear God, why would anyone feel like that? You really can't fully understand someone unless you walk in their shoes. Experience their pain and hurt. Where is his father? Did he have any siblings? He talks about finding the courage to be accepted by his peers. Did something go wrong at work? I pull out the ME's report. Nothing seems out of whack. I need to talk to Mrs. Blankenship. I put her number in my phone, so I can call her later to set up an appointment. Right now, I need to head home. I owe Andy the attention I didn't give him before. I put everything back in the folder and lock it in a cabinet and take off.

Chapter Three

When I get home, I find Stella and Patrick trying to play house with Mary, but she wants no part of it. She just turned three, and it's her way or the highway. Time stands still when she is watching *The Little Mermaid*, probably for the hundredth time. I love that she even put a tutu on Bacon, our rescue Pit Bull. The two of them are sitting in front of the TV, mesmerized. When that movie is on, nothing else matters. What I wouldn't do to be that age and clueless about the world we live in. I head into the kitchen and find MJ cooking.

"Hey, what's for dinner?" I ask.

She turns towards me with a vegetable peeler in her hand, like she's brandishing a weapon that she's planning to use on me. I'm trying not to laugh. "Did you know?"

The peeler gets closer to my face.

"Know what?" I know what she's asking, but I don't want to spill the beans if she doesn't really know. I swear life can be such a balancing act.

"Andy agreed to meet Stephen for dinner. That's where he is now."

"He mentioned it, but we didn't get to finish talking. What did he tell you?"

"They had unfinished business. What kind of bullshit is that?"

Her bottom lip quivers as she tries to hold back her tears. I take the peeler out of her hand and pull her into my arms. "Hey, babe, I know you want to protect him—we all do—but he's an adult. He knows what he wants and what he's willing to accept. You're his sister, and he looks to you for a lot of support, but now you need to give him some space. If he falls, we will be there to help pick up the pieces. That's what we always do." She pulls back and I wipe away her tears.

"I get all of that, really, I do. I know I'm not his mother, but you know what a setback he had physically when Stephen left him. What if that happens again? What if it's worse? Living with his Parkinson's is like jumping into a black hole in space. I finally feel like we've got some sort of handle on it and I worry what will happen if he gets stressed and upset."

"I worry too, but we will deal with it. Who knows, maybe they will work something out," I offer. She cocks her head and raises one eyebrow. That's her *quit-trying-to-feed-me-the-bullshit* look. "Okay, truth is, I was upset when he told me, but I have to support him the same way I support everyone else that comes to me for help or advice."

"Speaking of which, what did Father O'Neil want?"

"He wants me to look into something for him. It shouldn't take me too long to figure it out." I don't elaborate more, and she doesn't pry. She already knows I rarely share my work stuff with anyone. "What's for dinner?"

"You're barbecuing, and the kids are hungry, so let's get them fed first. I promised them they could go into the pool after dinner if they behaved."

Putting the pool in the yard was the best thing I ever did. MJ wasn't too thrilled about it, but in the long run, she was outnumbered.

It keeps the kids amused and all the neighborhood kids end up in our yard. My kids are always in sight. The bonus is, at the end of the day they are exhausted. They sleep through the night, and I get MJ time. I feel a twinge in my cock at the thought of alone time.

"Fitz, hello, where did you go off to?" She waves her hand in my face. I snap out of my daydream and follow her eyes as they roam down my body. She smiles and then pushes a plate of hot dogs and burgers my way. "The sooner you get them fed and in the pool, the closer we are to our quiet time." She shoots me a wink. I lean in and kiss her before heading out back. I don't need reminding how lucky I am.

The grill heats quickly, and before long, the smell fills the air. I'm wondering how Andy is making out. What if he needs an out and doesn't know how to do it? What if he doesn't have the courage to do it? Fear can be crippling if you let it in. I, of all people, know that. I'm tossing back and forth between the idea of texting or calling him. If he needs an out, I can give it to him. That's what best friends do. They help you even when they think you're making a huge mistake and then stick around to pick up the pieces. *Oh hell*; I call him. Four rings and then voice mail. Now I need to text him.

Me: Pick up the damn phone.

Andy: You know I'm out to dinner. Is everything okay?

Me: I'm calling you now, so answer the phone.

I hit redial, and he picks up after three rings.

"Is everything okay with Stella?"

"Of course, it is. I'm calling to see if you need an out."

"Really? Why would you do that?"

"Because that's what best friends do, Andy. Do you need an out?"

"You couldn't just text me?"

"No, and why are you arguing with me? What if it was him

texting that you're fine instead of you texting? I need to hear it from you." Why the hell do I have to explain everything?

"Look, if one of us were to be a walking *Dateline* episode, it would be you. I'm fine, but Stephen is on his way back from the men's room, so I need to go."

Before I can answer, he hangs up. I didn't see him when he left, so I do not know where he was going. This irks me to no living end. We are a family of iPhone users. The *Find My Friend* app saved MJ and Livy's life. God only knows what I'm going to do when my kids leave the house without me. I try not to invade anyone's privacy, but Andy pissed me off, so now all bets are off. I check up on him and it shows he's at Peter Luger's Steakhouse in Williamsburg, Brooklyn. That's Andy's favorite restaurant. I guess Stephen is pulling out all the stops. Now, normally, I would think nothing of jumping on Wanda and heading over there. I'd take a seat out of view and just keep an eye on things. That's the old me . . . the overprotective me. When you come close to death, you realize life is too short to waste a moment. I'm temporarily distracted by the smoke and flames coming out of the grill. When I lift the lid, everything is burnt. This, my friends, is a sign. I scrape everything off the grill, toss it in the trash, and head back inside. I hand MJ the empty plate.

"Umm, Fitz, what the hell happened to the dinner?"

"Babe, gather up the kids. It's Mickey Ds for dinner and then a special place for dessert." I place my finger over her lips. "Humor me, okay?"

She quickly gathers up the brood. When we finally make it to the car, she gets them in their car seats while I make a reservation for dessert. We go through the drive-thru and, of course, everyone wants to change up their meals. I can feel myself getting more and more exasperated. I guess the old me is never too far away. We get our order and we're finally on our way. While I drive, MJ gets to deal with the kids fighting over the toys from the happy meals.

"Do you want to tell me why we are eating in the car?"

"We have a reservation for dessert, and I don't want to be late."

"You're acting very weird, Fitz. Since when is dessert so important to you?"

"No worries, MJ. Everything is fine." I turn up the music. Luke Combs is singing, "When It Rains It Pours," and I'm singing right along with him. The kids are fighting over French fries, and MJ is the referee. Welcome to the good life, people. I wouldn't trade it for all the money in the world.

We pull up to Peter Luger and I'm about to get out when MJ grabs my arm. "You knew he was here. Don't even think of denying it. I know you tracked him. Why are you doing this?"

"I called him earlier to see if he needed an out."

"Oh, you should have said something sooner."

She turns to get out, and now I stop her. "MJ, he didn't need an out."

She's looking at me like I've got three heads. "Then why are we here?"

"It's the way he said it. And then he hung up on me."

"Oh, Fitz, what the hell am I going to do with you? Just face it and own it: Andy pissed you off, and now you want to piss him off. I swear sometimes I'm transported back to when you two would fight over your GI Joes only to turn around and set them on fire."

"Let's just be clear here. We weren't setting them on fire per se, we were simulating a battle."

She rolls her eyes, gets out and gets Stella and Patrick out, too. I scoop Mary up and sit her on my shoulders. I give the valet the key and wish him luck as we head inside. We are not a quiet bunch, but MJ warns the kids to use their library voice. That works for about two minutes. We are quickly seated. My eyes darting around the room. MJ leans in and whispers, "I don't see him. Are you sure he is here?"

I'm about to pull out my phone when the maître d' comes over and hands me a note. "I was told to give you this when you showed up and to tell you your dessert has been paid for."

I take the note. "Thank you, sir."

Fitz,

I know you better than you think. I didn't need an out. Believe it or not, I know what I'm doing. I love you both for always having my back. Enjoy your dessert and I'll see you at home.

A

"Okay, kids, order any dessert you want. The sky's the limit." I pass MJ the note and we both sit back and laugh.

Chapter Four

Andy

Twenty-Five years earlier

Before . . .

"Come on, Andy, it's about time you told them."

It's times like this when I wish he didn't live with us. He's always making me own up to stuff, yet, he has a vault of hidden shit. "Fitz, it's easy for you to say. I mean, after all, it's not your world that's being turned upside down."

"You're an idiot, Andy. It's the 90s, man; what's the big deal? It seems the only one who cares that you're gay is you."

"Sometimes I want to forget that I ever told you. You make it sound so simple. It's not, but you could never really understand unless you walked a day in my shoes. I'm made to feel different—period."

"Maybe you're right, but maybe you're making yourself feel different. Either way, I've always got your back, so don't worry. Do you want me to tell them?" he offers.

"No! That's the last thing I need." I wave my hands between us frantically. Fitz already got sent to the principal's office two times for fighting. He wouldn't say why, but I have a good idea he was defending me. I tried to tell him I can defend myself but he's very protective when it comes to family.

"Then don't be a wuss. Look, the worse thing that can happen is Mom says a few extra novenas for you. We could all use a few of those."

I know exactly how to shut him up. "I'll tell you what, how about I let you tell Mom and Dad that I'm gay. Then I can tell MJ how you have the hots for her." He gets a scowl on his face and the tops of his ears turn red. That's Fitz's tell. We all have one. When he's mad, his ears turn red.

"Shut the fuck up, Andy. You don't know shit."

He goes back to playing his Sega and totally tunes me out. I don't know why he thinks he's hiding his feelings for her so well or why he even thinks he has to. Some things with Fitz are a *don't-go-there—ever*—and my sister is one of them. Anyway, I thought about telling my parents sooner but then Dad got shot. He was one year shy of retiring. Being a cop was his life, yeah, he loves us, but the job was his world. He's only now adjusting to the fact that he'll never walk again. With Fitz completely in the gaming zone, I know the hemming and hawing over this decision with my best friend is over. I take in a deep breath. I guess he's right; there is no time like the present.

I head downstairs and find Mom in the kitchen putting dinner together. Dad's in his usual spot in front of the TV. "Mom, I need to talk to you and Dad about something."

"Is everyone okay? Are you in trouble?" she peppers me with questions. I smack my hand to my forehead. God, I wish there was an easier way of doing this. "Mom, everyone is fine, and I'm not in trouble. Let's go inside with Dad." I head into the living room with her on my heels.

"Pat, shut that stupid thing off. Andy has a problem."

I give up trying to tell her I don't have a problem. Well, in reality, I guess I have a problem. He quickly shuts the TV off and motions me to sit down. I decide to stand. "Mom, Dad, I don't know an easy way to say this, so I'm just going to come out with it. I'm gay." I slowly exhale and watch their faces for any sort of reaction—nothing. "Did you hear what I said? I'm gay."

"I'm not deaf, Andy, I just can't walk. Your mom said that you have a problem. If you don't tell me what it is, then I can't help you solve it." He throws his hands out as if to say "what gives?" and my mom looks at me like I am from another planet.

"I said I'm gay. I don't have a problem."

"So, is this the big secret that you think you were hiding so well from us?" His eyes are locked on mine, maybe looking for something.

"I thought you would be mad at me." My voice is barely above a whisper.

"Do you think Fitz and MJ had to come to us and tell us they are straight? No, so you don't have to tell us you're gay. Andy, at the end of the day, it's your business and yours alone, so do with it whatever you want. And Fitz, you might want to come out of the kitchen and stop lurking around."

I look over and Fitz steps into the doorway. His hands are in his pockets with a guilty look on his face. Mom gets up and gives me a hug. "Andy, your dad and I want you to be happy. That's all we've ever wanted for all our children." She kisses my cheek before heading back into the kitchen. Dad turns the TV back on, and their life goes back to normal. I've kept this secret for so long, the fear built up and ate away at me, wondering if there was something wrong with me. Why was I so different?

"But, Dad, wait, you're not mad at me?"

He lifts the remote and lowers the volume. "Son, why would I be mad? I'm a little sad that you've taken a road in life that I know won't be easy. However, at the end of the day, I know you didn't choose to be gay. You are who you are, and I love you. I've raised all my children to be strong, kind, and compassionate. Just remember, Andy, your family is here to support you. We just want you to lead a life that is filled with happiness." He picks up the remote and, once again, he's engrossed in the latest *Seinfeld* episode. Fitz and I head outside but not before grabbing a couple of cookies that Mom just took out of the oven. "I thought you were playing that stupid game?"

"I told you I would always have your back."

"I thought it would be harder than it was, Fitz."

"What the hell were you expecting . . . them to flip out? Oh, I know, maybe Mom could have Father O'Connor do some sort of exorcism on you." He gets hysterical laughing.

"You know, you're an ass."

"Just keeping it real."

We jump on our bikes and head off until dinner.

Ten years later

Today's my twenty-fifth birthday and I did the ballsiest thing I think I've ever done in my life. I actually asked a total stranger out on a date. Well, not really a *total* stranger, since he gets his car worked on at the shop where I work. After finding out that I passed my test for master mechanic on my birthday, no less, I figured it was a sign, so I decided to ask Stephen out for a drink. I've asked men out before, but no one in Stephan's caliber. I mean, he drives a top-of-the-line Benz. He's always dressed to the nines, and he's an attorney. The kicker is, he said yes! I figured my family wouldn't mind if we did the cake thing another day. Especially since Fitz is working and MJ is away at school. We decide on PDT (Please Don't Tell) on St. Marks Pl. in

Brooklyn. It's an odd place, but it has the best hotdogs. You haven't lived until you've had their Chang dog named after David Chang.

I check and re-check myself in the mirror at least a dozen times. I'm not sure why I'm so nervous. When I turn to leave, Fitz is blocking the doorway. "How long have you been standing there?"

"Long enough to know you must have a date tonight that you're nervous about. Who's the guy?"

I decide to steer the conversation away from my date. "I passed my master mechanic test."

"I told you not to worry. You should listen to me more. Oh, and by the way, happy birthday. Now, who's the guy, and where are you going?"

Sometimes he can be such a pain in my ass, but I understand him better than anyone, even himself. "He's a lawyer, and he gets his car serviced at the shop. As far as where we are going, I'm past the age of reporting my whereabouts. We're going out, Fitz."

He steps out of the doorway and his smirk is now gone. "Ouch, Andy, I don't need to be bitch slapped."

"You must be working a bad one because you're worse than usual." He loses himself in every case. This one has him in an overly protective prick mode.

"It's bad. I just stopped home to wish you a happy birthday before I head out."

"Will you be gone long?" I rarely ask him about his work, but this one really has him uptight.

"At least a couple of weeks, but I'll check in when I can. Have a good time tonight. Be safe."

"Okay, you too." I look at my watch. If I don't leave now, I'll be late.

I quickly head out and decide to take the train. It's a lot faster than driving and then trying to find a parking spot. Plus, I won't have to worry about drinking and driving.

I don't know why I'm nervous. It's not like I've never gone on a date before. It's just something about this guy has me intrigued. I walk into PDT and spot him at the bar. When he sees me, he smiles and, for the first time, I notice he has dimples. The closer I get to him, the more my heart races. Should I reach out to shake his hand? Too formal. Maybe a quick wave? An embrace—no, no, no—that's too much. What the fuck is wrong with me? When I reach the table, he stands up. I can't take my eyes off of his smile. *Damn.* I reach my hand out and he gives me a quick hug, instead, with a pat on my back.

"Happy birthday, Andy. Please, have a seat." He pulls a chair out for me before taking a seat.

"How did you know?"

"When I picked up my car today, I saw the birthday cake in the office. One of the girls offered me a slice and mentioned it was your birthday. I have to say, I was a little surprised when you asked me out. Do you do that often?"

The waiter interrupts us, and I order a local craft beer. "Once in a while. But truth is, I haven't in a long time."

"So, if you don't mind me asking, why me?"

"Whenever you bring your car in, I'm the one who does all the work on it. You know you can really judge someone by the inside of their car, and you intrigued me. Honestly, I didn't think you would say yes." I widen my eyes as if shocked. He throws his head back and laughs. The waiter drops off my beer and informs us that he will be back soon to get our order.

"So, tell me, what does the inside of my car say about me?"

"There is never anything out of place. Hell, you even have a Swiffer in your glove box. It always looks like your car just rolled off the showroom floor. A-type personality. Probably why you are an excellent attorney." There's that dimpled smile again.

"Thank you, I think. I requested you to work on my car because everyone said you're the best."

I take my bottle and tap it on his. "Today's a double celebration for me. Besides my birthday, I passed my test for master mechanic."

"Have you always wanted to be a mechanic?"

"Actually, I started out wanting to race cars. Then I got my hands dirty under the hood and I realized what I really love is taking the engines apart and tweaking them. I still love racing, but I do that with friends on the weekends. What about you? Have you always wanted to be an attorney?"

"I always loved the law and wanted to go into business law. I'm a right and wrong, black and white type of person. There was never any gray in my world. I started out my career in a small downtown firm. I figured I would get my feet wet and then apply to the big Wall Street firms. The firm I was with required all newbies to work an old case. It was an exercise to test us to look outside the box. I was given an old rape case and told to figure out if an appeal was warranted. He was sixteen but had the mental capabilities of a twelve-year-old. His emotional ability was even lower. There was no DNA evidence. The victim was fifteen, and the rapist used a knife to force himself on her. She was traumatized, which was understandable. The strongest thing in the case was the victim's identification. The kid had a court-appointed attorney who was new with a backload of cases. He talked the kid into taking a plea. This led to him being convicted of first-degree felony rape. He was sentenced to twenty-five years, but he would be eligible for parole after seven. Which, if he really did it, would be a good deal. But the kid didn't do it. However, none of that mattered; he took the deal."

He's weaving the tale like a master storyteller. In my mind, I'm envisioning him in a courtroom spinning the tale to a jury like they do on *Law and Order*. "Wow, so what happened?" I ask. He smiles and takes a sip of his beer. The suspense is killing me.

"I looked at the case and the only thing I could do was question the victim's identification. Yes, she was raped, but how positive was she that he was the one? I went to see her. I wasn't even sure she would talk to me, but she did. She was older and sometimes with time and age comes clarity. I knew it could go either way. When I spoke to her, she told me, at the time, her parents and the police pressured her to pick someone out of a line-up. She realized he really wasn't the one who raped her. She wanted to come forward but years passed, and she was afraid she could get into trouble. Long story short, the conviction was overturned. He was released from jail, and they expunged his record."

"So, it had a happy ending."

"No, not really. The damaged was already done. He couldn't function in mainstream society; he committed suicide. After that, I realized I didn't want to practice business law. I knew I wanted to work criminal law. That's enough about me. It's your birthday, and I want you to tell me more about you."

The waiter comes over to take our order. "Stephen, have you ever had the Chang Dog?"

"This is my first time here. Order whatever you want. I'm always game to try new things."

"You haven't lived until you tried the Chang Dog. It's named after David Chang. The Chang Dog is a hotdog that is wrapped in some kick-ass bacon, then it is deep fried, but it doesn't stop there. It's then put on a fresh baked bun and smothered with Chang's signature Momofuku kimchee. It's like an outer body experience."

"I'm a very boring visual eater. I look at a menu and order from the pictures. It must look like the picture, or I won't eat it. Quirky, I know."

"That's very sad. I love food and I love to cook. I have a friend who is a chef, and he always says, 'First you make love to the food with your eyes, then with the aroma, and, finally, with the taste.' You're really missing out on a lot."

He lifts his glass up to toast, "Here is to you, opening up my world to all different possibilities." When he taps his glass to mine, I have a tingle that runs down my spine.

Dinner comes and I make him close his eyes. He takes a bite and is blown away by all the new sensations. If nothing else comes of this night, I've at least opened his mind to all new possibilities. I've never had so much conversation in such a short amount of time. We finish up with a simple dessert and finally head out. Immediately, the sounds of the bustling city surround us which reminds me it's not just us in our own little world.

"This is an interesting area. Do you live around here?"

"No, I live in Bay Ridge near the shop. What about you?"

"I have a place on the upper east side. I don't suppose I could persuade you to come to my place for a nightcap?" He gives me a sheepish, sideways glance.

"Stephen, I had a wonderful night, and I hope we can get together again. But for now, I think I'll call it a night." I get really brazen. I lean in and kiss him. Just a simple brush of my lips on his. As I pull back, he puts his arm around my waist, pulls me close, and kisses me again. It's long and sensual. I want him. I *really* want him, but something is telling me to slow this down. I back up and there's that smile again. "Thank you again for a wonderful night." I step aside and turn to head toward the train. I want to look back, but yet I don't. What if he's already gone? Something is telling me to turn around. I'm about to make the trek down the subway steps. I stop, take a deep breath, and turn. That's when I see him watching me, his thumb gliding over his lips as if he can still feel mine on them. I wave, turn, and continue down the steps. I have to say, this was probably one of the best birthdays I've had in a long time.

Chapter Five

Five years later . . .

Fitz has been gone for eight long months. I think this is the longest he's ever been away. My sister has spiraled out of control since he left. She has gone down a path I never thought she would. She started dating a guy that owns a BDSM club and now he has gotten her entrenched into that world. He is an evil seed. Slowly, he was taking control of my sister's life. I didn't know what to do or how to handle it. I couldn't tell my parents; they would freak out. Hell, I freaked out. I thought of calling Fitz, but when he's working, he's all in. Telling him would be a distraction that could cost him his life. It's Stephen that has helped me keep it together. To keep my sister safe, I purchased the club. With one stipulation—he had to be gone. He took the deal and left town. I have her running the club. Is it an ideal situation—no—but it's better than the alternative. Eventually, I will find a way to get her out of there completely. Until then, I'm able to keep a close eye on her.

Fitz called Mom and let her know he's coming home next week.

He wants to be here for our wedding. Yes, Stephen and I are tying the knot, now that it's legal in New York. The wedding will be in three weeks. It's a simple one at the Justice of the Peace, with an intimate gathering of friends and family at my home. Not too long after Stephen and I met, I purchased my home. It's a brownstone around the corner from my parents. It was a total gut job but five years later, and it's officially done. Stephen has agreed to move in instead of buying something together. He understands my parents are aging and with MJ not living around the corner anymore, I don't want to be too far away. Family is my world; it's the way they brought me up.

I've been feeling very off lately. I can't seem to get a good night's sleep. Every day I seem to get light-headed. I can't have that crap happening to me while I'm at work. I was due for my yearly physical next month, but I went in early. I really thought it was just stress. Between the wedding and the renovations on the house, stress is a given. My stress level lately has been off the charts. Then, the doctor called me to come in for additional testing. I was a little nervous, but I shrugged it off. Today I went back to the doctor to go over all the results. Stephen wanted to go with me but today was closing arguments for a big case he's lead on. I didn't think it was a big deal, but then I felt like the rug was literally pulled out from under me. The world is officially off its axis. This can't be happening to me. *Why? God, why me?* Early onset Parkinson's: those words emblazoned in my brain. I left the doctor's office with an appointment to a neurologist, for confirmation of his diagnosis, and a handful of papers. The words kept swirling around my head. I'm supposed to get married in three weeks. Not anymore. Not after I looked it up on the internet and saw how bad this can really be. I'll give him an out. He deserves it. The ringing phone momentarily snaps me out of my fog. The screen lights up with my mom's name. I let it go to voicemail. Later when I listened to it, she is yelling for me to pick up the phone. She's worried; I was supposed to call her after the doctor. I'm not ready to talk to her, to anyone. *Why, God, why?* I try to be a good son, friend, and brother . . . damn, a good person. Why me? I hear the front door and look up at the clock in a panic. Day has turned into night and I haven't moved. Stephen's home. I need to get my shit together. I gather up the papers and shove them under the cushion I'm sitting on. I wipe my eyes and plaster a smile on my face.

"Hey, Andy, why are you sitting in the dark?"

"I must have fallen asleep," I answer quickly. He turns on the light. I squint and turn away.

"You are the worst liar in the world, which is another reason I love you. What's wrong? What are you trying to hide? Oh my God, did something happen at the doctor?" He drops his briefcase and races to my side.

I take a deep breath and dig down deep into my soul. "Stephen, everything is happening too quickly. I think I need a timeout. We need a timeout." He reaches for me and I turn my head away from him. "Don't, please." I know if I look at him, I'll lose it.

"We don't do timeouts, Andy. What we do is face everything together. If you think I'm going to let you push me away without a damn good reason, then you don't know me as well as you think!" He's yelling now and I'm trying to keep it together. But the images from the internet keep playing in my head. In the blink of an eye, I see myself heading to a nursing home, where I can live out my days having someone change my diapers. I'm only thirty-five fucking years old, and my body is going to betray me. "Stephen, it's for the best." My voice cracks before I can stop it. The tears start. I'm a grown-ass man and right now I have my head in my hands crying like a two-year-old. He pulls me into his arms. His grip around me is tight and, for the first time since I heard those words, I feel some comfort.

"I'm not going anywhere. When you're ready to talk, I'm here."

I lift my head and finally look him in the eyes. They always say so much. "I have early onset Parkinson's." His hands fall to his side. He closes his eyes for a moment and a look of sadness crosses his face. "Now, do you understand? I'm giving you an out, Stephen. You're young and you have your whole life in front of you. You just became a partner at the firm you always dreamed of working at. Your career is really taking off. I would never want to interfere in any of that. My world is going to change and not for the better. I wouldn't put you through any of that. Before you know it, I'll be a pathetic shell of myself. You don't need to deal with that."

"I'm going to give you a pass on trying to end things between us. I didn't just sign on for just the good times, Andy. Good or bad, I'm in it for the long haul. I love you and whatever happens, we will go through it together. You said it was early onset Parkinson's, so what do we do next?"

"I have an appointment with a neurologist to confirm and find out all my options."

"That's a great start. I mean, at your age, I'm sure there are things we can do now to keep it at bay. Who knows, ten years from now they might have a cure for it. I think the first thing we need to do is contact The Michael J. Fox Foundation and find out what our options are. I have some clients that have put large donations to the organization in their wills. They really do a lot of good. Right now, Andy, you are in control of the disease. The disease doesn't control you. We need to learn what we can do to keep it that way. Did you tell your parents yet?"

"No, I want to wait until Fitz gets back next week. They will look to him for support."

"I agree with you, but I'm not sure how you are going to keep this from them until then. What about MJ?"

I feel all the color drain from my face. "She is supposed to stop over here tonight after work. I'm going to have to tell her. Until Fitz gets home, I will swear her to secrecy." I pull all the papers out from under my cushion and pass them to him. "Since you're not going anywhere, you might as well look at all of this." He takes the papers and puts them on the coffee table.

"There will be plenty of time for that later. Right now, we need to eat. I'll heat up leftovers from last night. It's not cooking, but it's the best I can do."

"We can eat later. Right now, I could use a long, hot shower. Why don't you come with me?" I don't have to explain. He gets it. I need to fall apart in the safety of his arms.

I don't know what I did in life to find someone who loves me so deeply. When I look over at the clock and realize MJ should have been here by now. I quietly slip out of the bed, careful not to disturb Stephen. When I get downstairs, I find her sitting on the sofa with all the pamphlets spread out in front of her. My heart is in my throat. As I step further into the room, her eyes meet mine and she's been crying.

"I'm sorry you had to find out like this." I wave my hand over all the pamphlets before I try to gather them all up. "I was waiting up for you, but I must have fallen asleep. Say something, MJ, please."

"What do you want me to say? I will do whatever you need me to do. Is there a treatment plan or something? Did you tell Stephen? What about Mom and Dad?" She's peppering me with questions, fast and furious.

"Slow down, please. I just found out today. The only one who knows is Stephen. I'm going to wait till Fitz gets home to tell Mom and Dad. In the meantime, I'm going to see a specialist and find out what my options are," I explain. She gets up and pulls me into a tight hug.

"When is your appointment with the specialist?"

I pull back and wipe away her tears. I know she wants to be strong for me and I love her for it, but Fitz and I have always protected her, and we always will, no matter what. I don't think I could handle her having to protect me. "Tomorrow morning."

"I'm going with you and no arguing." She turns and heads into the kitchen. Sometimes she's like a whirlwind.

"MJ, it's three o'clock in the morning. What are you doing?"

"Putting up a pot of coffee. I want to make a list of questions for the doctor. If we wait till we are there, you'll forget everything. Now sit." She pulls out a chair and gives me the death look. It's the look she has given Fitz and me whenever she wanted her way. We always end up doing whatever she wants, and I can't help but laugh.

"Mind telling me what's so funny?"

"I love you. You're the best little sister any guy could ever ask for." I hear the front door open and I'm out of my chair in a second. I grab the wooden dowel by the back door. "Stay right here and call the police," I whisper. I hear the floorboards creek right outside the kitchen. With the pole like a bat, I take a swing at whatever is around the opening. I connect and feel the vibration of the wood in my hands.

"Damn it, Andy, what the fuck is wrong with you?"

"Fitz! What the fuck are you doing here? Are you trying to give me a heart attack? Did I hurt you?" He's rubbing his arm where I hit him.

"No, but I'm sure I'll have a bruise by morning. I got a text from Stephen to come home ASAP. I didn't want to wake up Mom and Dad. His message was kind of cryptic. Is everyone okay?"

We sit down and MJ gets us coffee. "I can't believe he texted you. I didn't want to bother you."

"Andy, just spit it out. What's wrong?"

"I have early onset Parkinson's." I put it out there and the words hang in the air. He looks from me to MJ and back again.

"Okay, now what? I mean, you always treated your body like a temple. That should count for something. You're young and it's not a death sentence. We'll find you the top doctor for this. Whatever the cost, I'll cover it. I don't want you worrying about anything."

He's not my brother by blood, but he is in every way it counts. "We were just going to make up a list of questions for the neurologist."

"Okay, let's do this." He grabs the pad and pen and pushes it towards MJ.

We spend the next hour listing everything under the sun. I think we have a good start. I'm looking at him and for the first time, I notice the solemn look on his face. "Fitz, are you okay?"

"You're worried about me? I'm fine, Andy, just exhausted. This case was a bad one. When kids are involved, it destroys me. I just need a little time to unwind and recharge my soul. Now tell me, what's your greatest fear here?" He passes me the pad.

"Wearing diapers," I admit without missing a beat. MJ almost chokes on her coffee and Fitz is laughing. "What's so funny? I don't want to lose my man card."

"Andy, I need you to fight this disease as hard as you can. You do that and I promise you, if you end up in diapers, I'll take you out back and shoot you myself."

"That is a promise I'm going to hold you to." We all laugh. I look at my watch and realize it hasn't even been twenty-four hours since I got the news. In that time, so much has changed. Yet, the one thing that never will change is the support of my family. I really am blessed.

Chapter Six

Andy

Now . . .

I walk into Peter Luger's and Stephen is waiting at the bar. This is the first time I've seen him since he left me a goodbye note. He tried to push me to choose him over my family. He turns and smiles. My stomach does a flip at the sight of him. It's been years since I've seen him, yet, in my heart, it feels like it was yesterday. I'm willing my feet to move, but nothing is happening. I snap out of it and as I head toward him, he stands up. I'm instantly reminded of all the time we spent together. He pulls me into a quick hug. He feels so good. Dear God, please give me strength.

"Andy, thank you for coming. I wasn't sure you would."

"Why? Because of the shitty way you ended things with me?" Damn it! I don't want to sound bitter.

"Ouch, but I guess I deserve that." He turns a bar stool toward him. "Please, have a seat. Tell me about your life. I know it's been a while. Are you dating?"

"Always right to the point. That's probably why you're such an excellent attorney. I've had a few dates but, honestly, I'm not sure what I want. What about you?"

He swirls the liquid in his glass, no doubt hoping if he stares at it long enough, the right words will appear. The bartender puts a cold beer down in front of me. "Your friend ordered it for you."

I take a sip and glance over to Stephen. "It's okay if you have. I never expected you to remain single." He lifts his eyes to meet mine. My chest feels heavy.

"I've been on a few different dating sites recently. It seems that's the only way to meet someone anymore. I've been seeing a very nice guy for the past three months. He wants to take it to the next level, you know . . . something more exclusive."

"So, is that why you called me? To see if it's really over, or are you looking for my approval?" There is always a method to his madness, and I wouldn't be surprised if that were the case.

"I honestly don't know. I just felt that we never really had closure."

I take a few slow breaths. It's something I've learned to do when I feel stress building up. It helps my shaking and right now, I feel a burning sensation up my spine. My fingers are trembling. I clasp my hands together and put them in my lap. "Closure? I hate that word. What exactly do you need closure on? The fact that you walked out on me, your husband, and you did it with a letter. Or maybe the fact that I came home, and you had cleared out everything. You didn't even leave me a fucking chair! What type of closure are you looking for?"

At that moment, my phone rings and it's Fitz. I hit end. It automatically rings again. Then, he follows it with a text message.

"Apparently, it's important that someone speaks to you. I need to use the men's room; you can take care of that call."

He gets up and heads to the men's room. I quickly text Fitz and tell him I'm fine, but he's not buying it. Sometimes I want to kick his ass like I used to do when we were kids. The phone rings again.

I give up and answer it. I convince him I'm fine and hang up just as Stephen comes back.

"Is everything okay?"

"Yes, Fitz was checking in. Everything is fine."

"I heard what happened to Fitz, that he was buried alive and survived. I told you MJ can deal with all that shit, but I refused to."

"This is not about them. It's about us and your need for *closure*." I say the word long and slow as it grates on my nerves.

"Look, Andy, I knew if I waited to tell you in person, I would have caved. You always said one thing you loved about me was my strength, but when it comes to you, I have none. I was so mad at you. We had a plan, and you didn't stick to it. Kids were never in our plan. And it's like I had no say in the matter."

My grip on my beer is so tight I feel like I could crush the bottle with my bare hand. "I think you have a selective memory, Stephen. You told me exactly how you felt and right before you used my disability against me. I could deal with a lot, but that was the nail in the coffin. You broke my heart when you did that, but you know that already. Couples are supposed to grow together. We might have started out thinking we didn't want kids, but life changes and, unfortunately, you didn't change with it. You know the old saying "we make plans and God just laughs" well, not everything is black and white. So, why don't you tell me why you're really here tonight?"

"I want to know if we have a shot." He reaches over and takes my hand firmly in his. I can feel my heart literally skip a beat. I take a deep breath and pull my hand back. Does he think that I'll just jump at the chance? Or maybe because I'm disabled, no one but him would ever want me. The lingering doubts will always be there.

"Stephen, even if I put aside my hurt because I believe, in time, we could possibly work things out, the bottom line is: I'm not your difference."

He pulls his stool closer.

"I don't understand. What the hell do you mean by difference?"

"I want to be the difference between casual and intense. I don't want someone who's going to play it safe. I want to be someone's aha moment, not an afterthought. Someone who can see past my Parkinson's and not use it as a weapon against me. That's what I want. When you pity someone who has a disability, you disempower them. I want someone who's going to embrace being a parent as much as I have. Stephen, I'm someone's dad. Do you know how intense that is? How powerful that is? Whatever I say and do matters to someone other than me. I have to lead by example. Stella is my world, and I can't imagine my life without her. Unfortunately, I can imagine my life without you in it. I had no choice. I had to pull all the strength I could find deep down into my soul the day I came home and found you gone with nothing but a note. I made it through the hurt and the pain that gutted me for so long. Now, I can honestly say I'm okay. I'm not saying this to be mean or spiteful; you know me better than that. This whole time, you never even asked me how she's doing. That's what I mean by difference, Stephen. I want someone in my life that knows the difference between having a life that revolves only around him or her and a life that can encompass my child. I actually feel sorry for you. You'll never experience life until you see it through the eyes of a child. I wish you all the best, I really do, but our lives are very different now." I get up and he jumps up and pulls me into a hug. It takes all of me not to give into his embrace.

"Andy, you're giving me a million reasons why I should walk away from you now. But, babe, there is really only one reason in the world why I can't walk away. I still love you. I have always loved you. That never changed. Come home with me, please. I know if you give me the chance, I can change your mind."

Begging is unbecoming and only cements my decision. "Good luck, Stephen. But now, I'm the one who needs to walk away from you." I pull out of his embrace. This is by far one of the hardest things

I've ever had to do. I turn and walk out. On our first date, I turned around, looked back at him, smiling. Now, I leave and never look back. Doing the right thing isn't always the easiest. In fact, it's usually the hardest.

I love my family, even though they can be overbearing at times. I glance at my watch and figure right about now they are enjoying dessert. Seeing Stephen brought back a flood of memories and feelings that I've tried to forget. I realize now that I was wrong to do that. Yes, our marriage ended badly, but there were so many good times . . . times in my life when I was healthy and happy. However, seeing him tonight made me realize I can't go back. It's been said that time heals. I don't think that's true. Time makes the terrible memories move to the back of the bus and the good ones take their place. They never really disappear. It's like when you move away. The bad reasons for the move fade out in time. Then you go back, and all the bad stuff rises to the surface. You remember why you moved.

It was the same tonight. When I walked in and saw him for the first time, my heart skipped a beat. However, after talking to him for a while, I realized nothing has changed for him. Truth be told—nothing has changed for me, either. I drew my line in the sand when he left me. Tonight, he needed closure before he could fully move on. I'm happy that he found someone who is giving him what he needs. I told him I forgave him a long time ago, and I wished him all the happiness in the world. It was the truth; I don't hold a grudge. It's nothing but a waste of time, and who knows how long I have. Now, I need to take my own advice and move on. This time, I know it will be different. When I first met Stephen, I wasn't sick. When I found out I had Parkinson's, I pushed him away. He wouldn't leave. He said he signed on for the good and the bad. Unfortunately, he didn't sign on for a kid. When Stella came into my life, it changed. She gave me purpose, the purpose I didn't realize I was missing in my life. She taught me that it's okay to be different. I wish her mom had lived, so she could see how wonderful and compassionate her daughter is. I know she would be proud. Stephen is too self-centered to have a child. I genuinely meant it, tonight, when I wished him all the best. Tomorrow, I will put myself out there. I pour myself another whisky and hold it up. "Here's to moving on, Stephen," I toast to what was and what could have been had his heart not been so closed off.

I'm wallowing in my last pity party for what was. Jacob is fast asleep by the door, waiting for Stella to come home. He opens his eyes and sits up with his stumpy tail moving like a metronome in time with the music. Any minute, that door will fly open and my daughter will come barreling through. Sure enough, the door opens and Fitz comes in with Stella fast asleep in his arms. He passes her to me, and I put her to bed. Jacob crawls in and rests his head on her belly. She's my difference. Before I head out of her room, I take an extra minute to look at her. I'm a lucky man that God brought us together, and I never take that for granted. Fitz is waiting for me in the living room. I can't say I didn't expect it.

"How was your dessert?" I'm trying not to laugh. It's not every day that I can get one over on him.

"We all had the Luger's Special: "Holy Cow" Hot Fudge Sundae. You spent a small fortune, and it was wonderful."

"I would expect nothing less." I take a seat while he pours himself a whiskey. He settles in across from me. I feel like I'm in the hot seat and he's going to slam me with questions.

"First, Andy, I want to apologize. Not for showing up at the restaurant, because I would do that all over again. I didn't give you the time and attention you deserve when you came to talk to me about Stephen. In my defense, I see red when his name comes up. I can't help it."

"I understand, but I can't hold on to the hurt. It's not productive. Besides, we're supposed to set an example for our children."

He looks everywhere around the room but at me, like he's uncomfortable. "Do you want to talk about what happened tonight?"

"Stephen joined a few dating sites trying to find a long-term relationship. I think he wanted to see me again and make sure, in his mind, that it was really over."

"What did you think when you saw him again?"

I drain the last of my whiskey, using liquid courage to honestly answer his question. "When I walked into the room, all the memories came flooding back. Not just the good ones. He made some overtures, I guess, to see if our split was permanent."

"And was it? I mean, in your mind, did you know?"

"He asked me to go home with him. I was tempted, remembering all the times his touch made my heart skip a beat. After all, I'm only human, Fitz."

"So, why didn't you take it further?"

"Stella. He never asked about her the entire time we were there. He never asked how our parents were or MJ. The only thing he said was, and I'm quoting here, 'I heard Fitz was buried alive and he survived. I told you MJ can deal with all that shit, but I refused to.' He sealed his fate with that."

He gets up and pours another whiskey. Good thing he only has to walk across the street. "Have you decided what you're going to do next? I mean, you've gone on a couple of dates, but don't you think it's time to put yourself out there? You know, the older we get, the faster time goes."

I laugh and I can't stop. "Fitz, sometimes you are like an old, wise warrior or something. Anyway, I've decided to join a dating site. Hopefully, not the same one as Stephen. I want Stella to see that love is love. It can be pure and beautiful. Right now, the only couples she ever gets to see interact is you and MJ and Travis and Olivia. She does have Mom and Dad, but that's different."

"You're going to have to come up with someone pretty fantastic to top MJ and me. Have you talked to Stella about any of this?"

"If you mean that I'm gay, yes. I've explained to her that love comes in all shapes, forms, and sizes. I think if I meet someone and get to where I want to bring him around my daughter, she'll be a little older and more mature."

"Have you told MJ any of this?"

"She knows I've been thinking about it. She's been sending me some of the better sites to join. By the look on your face, I'm guessing she never told you."

"No, but I respect your privacy." His brow unfurls.

"Thank you. I really thought I wasn't ready to put myself out there. Honestly, I didn't know if I would ever be. I really thought Stephen had the best of me."

"So, what changed?"

I'm running through all the events of tonight in my head like an old-time movie reel, trying to figure out how to explain my feelings to him. "When I came to you this morning and told you about meeting Stephen, and you lost your shit on me, I realized you were right." I can't help but laugh at the shit-eating grin on his face. "Yeah, Fitz, I'm saying it—you were right. You can wipe that grin off your face anytime now."

"I think I'll savor it for a bit. Anyway, continue, please." He waves his hand to push me along.

"At the end of the day, I've come to realize that the terrible memories fade to black and I'm left with all the happy times. I can forgive him. Hell, I did forgive him a long time ago. I just can't have him in my inner circle anymore. It's not good for me and it certainly isn't good for my daughter. Stella and me . . . we're a team. I'm supposed to be teaching her about life but, truth be told, she's teaching me."

"Well, it sounds like I was worried for nothing, but please promise me that you'll be careful. I was never a fan of dating sites but I understand that, in today's world, it's become the norm."

"Don't worry. I'll be fine. But, if you don't get your ass home, you won't be." With that, he gets up and heads out the door.

Chapter Seven

Fitz

By the time I get home, everyone is asleep. Just as well, since my mood has soured. I'm proud of the way Andy stood up for himself tonight. The more I think about Stephen, the more pissed I get. I never realized how selfish he could be. He does not know what a real family is all about. If Andy would have gone back to him, I really think it would have put a wedge between us. Not that Andy would have wanted that, but sometimes people are manipulated into things they never thought they would do. Before I go to bed, I head upstairs to check on the kids. I try to be home when it's bedtime. I missed my goodnight kisses and hearing their nightly prayers tonight. I'm sure this has added to my pissy mood. When we first got Bacon, he would sleep with Patrick. After Mary was born, Bacon moved to the hallway between both rooms. I check on Patrick and, of course, he's in his usual position: on his side, with his butt up against the headboard. No matter how many times I move him, he always ends up in the same position. I tuck him in and give him a kiss before heading into Mary's room. She is a princess, living in a room that has exploded in pink everything. Although, now that she's discovered *The Little Mermaid*, I'm sure this will all change. She just moved up to a big girl's bed. She sleeps in the middle of the bed and never moves. I try to be as quiet as possible because she is a light sleeper. She stirs when I kiss her forehead after I tuck her in. Before I leave the room, I make sure she is asleep. I head into our bedroom, and I find MJ asleep with her kindle clutched in her hand. I gently pull it out and give her a kiss before heading into the shower.

The water heats quickly and I'm soon lost in my thoughts. This day has been crazy. So much personal stuff. And now with this fresh case, I'm going to have to dig deep into someone else's personal life. They aren't here to defend themselves, so a lot of it will be assumption. Suicide cases are sometimes the hardest ones. The family doesn't want to believe it, but it doesn't change the fact that their loved one is dead. I know Father O'Neil was trying to link these deaths together, but the chance of that being fact is little to none. If Arman Blankenship took his own life, I need to figure out why. No one wakes up one day and decides to kill themself. There is usually a buildup of circumstances. The water runs cold, and that's my sign that I'm done. When I pull the curtain back, MJ is leaning against the sink, her arm outstretched with a towel for me. "Thank you. You were fast asleep. What happened?"

"You happened. I turned, and you weren't there. What happened with Andy?"

"He made me proud tonight. You know that saying, 'better the devil you know than the devil you don't?' It would have been the easy way to take Stephen back. Instead, he wants more. He deserves more. You know, I was thinking back to the day that he found out he has Parkinson's. The three of us sat at the table and came up with a plan. Stephen was upstairs sleeping the whole time. Andy never said he wanted Stephen involved in any of our decisions. It was just us family. Who knows, maybe even then the handwriting was on the wall and none of us saw it. Either way, I'm glad he fights so hard to have a normal life. Why shouldn't he? Plus, I don't want to have to shoot him anytime soon." I lift her up and she wraps her legs around my waist as my towel falls to the floor. "You're beautiful, babe." She brushes her lips gently on mine. Sex with MJ is my more, it's beyond typical and mundane. After all these years, it's unexpected and unpredictable. She loves me deeply. She leans in and kisses me. My lips instantly part, giving her all of me. She has one of Mary's pink hair ties trying to tame her wild mane. I slip it out and run my fingers through her hair. She holds on tight as I make my way back to our bedroom. I need to get out of my own head. The best way to do that is surrendering myself to her. I let her take the lead and do whatever she wants. I crawl into bed without breaking our connection. In an instant, she has me on my back while she's kissing my neck. She takes my hands and holds them above my head. "Now keep them there or I'll get out your cuffs."

I have to always touch her. It's what keeps me grounded, so this is especially hard for me. She's nipping and kissing her way down my chest. She takes my nipple in her mouth. It's so warm and comforting until she grates it between her teeth. The tug makes my cock stand at attention. She works her way to the other one. I'm usually the boob man in the family, but right now, what she's doing is driving me insane. "MJ, that's so. . ." she nips at my nipple. I'm trying to stifle my scream. My fist flies down and slams into the mattress. "Oh, dear God, more, please!"

"Hands up, now."

I trail my fingers up her back before I raise my arm above my head. Keeping them there is so hard. Her soft kisses are everywhere, and I don't know how much more of this I can take. My entire world is MJ, loving her. She wraps her hand around my cock as she swirls her tongue around the top. She's teasing me, up down, up down, then another swirl around the top. I'm teetering on the edge, and then she does the throat bump. I can endure a lot, well, except for that bump. She knows what it does to me and she takes great pleasure in watching me come undone. I've lost all control. I reach down and pull her up as I flip us over.

"Now, I'm on top and in control."

"Do you want me to put my hands above my head like I made you do?"

"No! I want your hands all over my body as I take us both to the promise land." I enter her slowly, savoring every inch that my cock is buried inside of her. When I'm all the way in, I take a long, slow breath before I move. I'm trying to prolong what I know is coming, but when she reaches up and tweaks my nipples, I lose it. I get on my knees and flip us over again. "Ride me, babe, hard." That's all the direction she needs. Her red mane is everywhere. She takes my hands and puts them on her boobs. That's it for me. "MJ, I can't hold back!" Her body flushes, and I know she's there, too. We're both trying not to scream. It's something you learn when you have children. You want to keep them asleep, so you stifle your yelling during sex. She collapses on top of me. Her breathing is slowing down. I try to move but she's not budging. Using my feet to get the covers (yes, I am really that gifted), I pull them up. Before too long, she's purring like a kitten.

Chapter Eight

Fitz

I'm usually the first one up and the last one to bed. However, after last night, my body is not ready to greet the world, yet. I would love nothing more than to lie in bed and relive last night. Unfortunately, I have work to do. Plus, there are two very active children that make it their business to never let me sleep in.

"Daddy." Bang, bang, bang, as if on cue. "Mommy said you better come downstairs before Bacon eats your breakfast." Bang, bang, bang.

"Okay, Patrick, tell her I'm on my way." We taught him to knock rather than barging right in. Now he just keeps knocking. He's a work in progress, people. I hear him yelling my answer to MJ as he heads downstairs. I'm reminded when we were kids. Mom would ask one of us to tell Dad dinner was ready. Instead of going into the other room to get him, we would yell. She would, in turn, yell at us that she could have done the same thing. I always thought—well, then why didn't you? That is until I became a parent. They say life goes in a full circle and, eventually, we become our parents. The thought makes me laugh as I head into the shower.

As I head downstairs, the wonderful smell of a fresh pot of coffee greets me. The kids are running through the rooms playing an in-door version of tag that Andy taught them. I grab my cup of coffee and the *Post*. MJ glances up at me from her coffee cup. She's biting her bottom lip, like she's trying to control her laughter. The look is causing my cock to stand up and salute. I mouth "What?" She shakes her head and looks down at her coffee. When I open the *Post* and see that Mary has colored everyone's hair red! I quickly thumb through the paper. There is not one page she hasn't colored. I glance over the top of the paper at MJ and she begins to laugh.

"Fitz, you have to admit; she is talented." She has a satisfied smile that parents get when they are proud of their children.

"When did she find the time to do this?"

"While I was making breakfast."

"Mary Elizabeth!" I bellow just as Patrick runs into the kitchen.

"Oh no, middle name! You're in deep crap now, sissy pants."

"Patrick, what did I tell you about calling your sister that name?" MJ reprimands him.

"Sorry, Mom, but she is in trouble."

Mary walks into the kitchen with her hands on her hips, and her chin held high. Lord, help me, I'm doomed before she even starts. "Hi, Daddy, I love you."

Deep breaths, Fitz. "Why did you color in Daddy's newspaper?" I ask her.

"Day have my hair now." She has a hard time with the letter t, so sometimes they come out like the letter d.

"Maybe they didn't want your hair," I offer her the possibility.

She flips her hair from one side to the other. "Day love my hair, just like you do." She leaps into my lap and gives me a kiss. That's it; color wherever you want.

"Yes, princess, Daddy loves your hair." She laughs, turns around and slides off my lap. She takes off running with Bacon running behind her. This right here, my friends, is my nirvana.

"MJ, I've got to head into the office today. I should be home early, but without having Hudson in the office much, everything is falling behind."

"Fitz, I would come in and help but Olivia should be coming home today. I'm going to go shopping for them. I'll make some meals, too, so they don't have to worry."

"Thank you. Don't worry about filling in for Hudson. Sal put an ad for an administrative assistant on a job site. He has been interviewing all week. Hopefully, he can find someone that fits in with our brand of crazy." I pull her in for a kiss before I head out. "I'll text you later what time I'll be home. Love you."

It's a beautiful day to ride Wanda. Usually, I would walk the couple of blocks or cut through the alley, but I need to go see Mrs. Blankenship about her son. When I get to the office, Sal is already there in the conference room. I wave as I head to the file cabinet, but he waves me in. "I didn't mean to interrupt. I needed to pull a file."

"No problem, Fitz. This is Nathan West. He's here about the job."

He waves. Now, don't get me wrong; I'm as laid back as the next guy but get up and, at least, offer to shake my hand. Manners seem to be a thing of the past. I give Sal the look that he knows all too well. "Nice meeting you, but I've got to get back to work." I pull my file and go to my desk. As I pass Hudson's desk, I'm reminded of how much I miss the kid. I pull everything out of the file, spreading it out on my already-cluttered desk. Talk to me, Arman. Tell me what would make a prominent doctor commit suicide? This last note to his mother doesn't match with the other notes. I look up as Nathan leaves. He doesn't say goodbye, not even a wave.

"Fitz, you have to stop finding fault with everyone that applies for the job. No matter whom we hire, no one will be Hudson. We have to be happy about her decision and be supportive. If we keep pulling her in here to help, we are just packing on the guilt she already feels for leaving us."

"Is that little speech for me or you?"

"I have one more applicant coming in tomorrow evening at six. Try to be here for it."

I give him a salute. He shakes his head and walks away, mumbling under his breath. I have that effect on people. The first thing I need to do is look through Arman's stuff. I dial his mother's number. She picks up on the first ring.

"Hello, Mrs. Blankenship, I'm Fitz—."

"—I know who you are," she cuts me off. "I've been waiting for you to call."

"Can I come by, so we can talk?"

"Yes, I'll be here waiting for you. Do you have my address?"

"Yes, ma'am, I'll be there shortly."

She hangs up, but I'm left with a strange feeling. I shake it off and head out. Her home is only a few blocks from the church. It always amazes me how so many people can live in the same parish, yet we don't know each other. When I pull up to her house, she's waiting on the front stoop for me. "Hello, Mrs. Blankenship, it's nice to meet you. Although, I wish it could be under better circumstances." I shake her hand and when I do, she wraps both hands around mine.

"Please, call me Joan. Let's go inside. After you called, I put up a fresh pot of coffee."

When we head inside, it's the same layout as my parents' house. Most of these brownstones are the same unless they've been renovated. "I understand from Father O'Neil that you have some doubts about the way your son died. Do you have any reason to believe otherwise?" I know what Father O'Neil told me, but I want to hear it directly from her, in her own words.

"My son would never take his own life. Didn't you read his letters? The last one—that wasn't my son."

"In today's world, writing letters is not a common thing."

"He knows how much I love writing and receiving letters. It's a dying art. They don't even teach the kids cursive in school anymore. How are they expected to sign their names, with a big X?"

"Wow, I didn't know they stopped teaching it."

"I retired last year. I was a math teacher for twenty-eight years. Times have changed. So much so that I lost my desire to teach. That's when I knew it was time to retire. It thrilled my son that I finally hung up my chalk, as he would say. He wanted to take me to some places that he traveled to. I'm a widow, so I was looking forward to our first trip. He was going to take me to Poland. We still have family there. I can't believe he's gone." She is constantly wringing her hands. I watch what people do, not just what they say. Sometimes I can learn more about what they are hiding or what they fear.

"Where is all your son's stuff? I would like to look through it." She gets up and I follow her down the hall.

"I cleaned out his condo in Manhattan and put everything that I thought was important in his old room. All the furniture I donated to the church's annual yard sale." She opens the door and there are boxes stacked neatly in the corner of the room. I look through them and find his laptop. "Do you mind if I take this?"

"You can have whatever you think you need. I want answers, Fitz, and I'm not giving up until I get them." I also find a journal; those are usually goldmines.

"Do you have his password for the computer?" So many people don't realize what their loved ones have to go through when they die. The simple steps they can take to make life easier.

"Yes, Arman kept a book with his passwords and important papers in a firebox. I've got it in my room. I'll be right back." She leaves and I continue to look through the boxes. I find a photo of two men at some sort of carnival. They seem happy. She comes back into the room. Her eyes instantly go to the photo I'm holding.

"That's Arman on the left with his best friend, Matt Daniels."

"Was your son in a relationship with Matt?"

"No. They were best friends, that's all. Arman met someone recently on a dating site. He was really upbeat about it. That's why none of this makes any sense to me. He was so happy."

"Do you mind if I hang on to this photo?"

"That's fine. Just get to the truth, please." At the end, her voice shook a little. I take her hand and give it a gentle squeeze.

"Okay, I think I have enough to start. I promise I will let you know as soon as I find out the truth, no matter what it is."

I head out and load everything into my saddlebags. When I turn around to get on Wanda, I look up at the house. Joan is on the stoop, wiping away her tears. My heart breaks for her. There is nothing worse than not knowing.

Chapter Nine

Andy

I'm very blessed that Stella is a pleasant child, yet, getting out the door on time for school is always stressful. I usually walk Stella and Patrick to school while MJ picks them up. However, I knew MJ would be busy helping Olivia and Travis with Piper, so I volunteered to take over for the time being. Besides, some of the best conversations with these kids happen at these times. Today's conversation was a real doozy.

"Uncle Andy, Mommy said you have to get a life. Where do you go to get a life?"

I can't tell him I want to kick his mother's ass. "I have a life, Patrick, it's just different from what your mom thinks it should be."

Stella stops walking and looks up at me. "Daddy, are you going to go to the same place you got me to get a life? Will I be able to stay in your life?"

I crouch down next to her and kiss her trembling hands. "You are my life. Never doubt that." She throws her arms around me. She's lost so much at such a young age. I know that sometimes she needs reassurance that she's always wanted. When we get to the school, she always takes Patrick's hand and walks with him into the building. He's younger than her, but that doesn't matter. They are very protective of each other. It's a year-round private Catholic school that goes from kindergarten through high school, so they will have each other's back, always.

After dropping them off, I make a stop at the bakery before I get to my dad's house. Mom will yell, but I always tell him, "Life is short; eat the cannoli." When I get to the house, Hudson is just leaving. She came to us when she needed help. We took her in and now she's part of the family for life. "Hey, I thought you were on the four to twelve shift?" She pries open the box from the side and pulls out a cannoli.

"I'm going by the office first. Sal's been trying to hire someone. Fitz doesn't like anyone. Thanks for the treat!" She heads off down the street. I yell out for her to be careful. She gives me a wave as she's shoving her cannoli in her mouth. Mom has finally accepted the fact that Hudson is a cop. It has not been easy on any of us, especially Mom. For a while, Hudson would come home every night to find her clothes folded by the front door. That was Mom's way of dealing with it. She finally realized that Hudson is happy. Half the battle in life is finding your happy. I head upstairs. If I want to find my father, all I have to do is follow the noise from the television. I pass him the box of cannoli. "Hey, Dad, you're short one. Hudson snagged one on her way to work." While he digs in, I grab the coffee for us.

"Did the kids get to school okay?"

"Yes, but not before Stella hit me with some hard questions. I've got to remind MJ not to talk in front of the kids about my personal life. It seems to interest them more than it should."

"Well, now that you mentioned it, what happened with Stephen last night?"

"Does the entire world know I met up with him?" He puts his cannoli down and gives me the death look.

"I'm not the entire world son; I'm your father. I take an interest in all my kids' lives. Just wait until Stella is older and boys start hanging around. You're going to be a basket case. Now, back to what happened." He never misses a beat.

"He was on a fishing expedition. Basically, he wanted to know if I wanted to get back with him before he moved on to a more exclusive relationship." He's not saying anything, which is very unnerving. "Well, aren't you going to hit me with a million questions?"

"Nope. I trust you. I know you would always put your daughter first. Anyway, I'm sure Fitz was all over you about this. Besides, Andy, if you made a stupid move, MJ would beat your ass." His laughter is not amusing me right now.

"You know, I thought about it all night. It's been a couple of years since he walked out. I'm sure he put himself out into the dating world right away, so why now?"

"Guilt, son, is a funny thing. It can make you do things you never thought you would. He feels guilty about how he ended it with you. He's a good-looking, successful man. I'm sure he's not at a loss for companions. The thing is, Andy, you can have all the money, looks and stuff in the world but, at the end of the day, you take your boxers off the same as any other man: one leg at a time. When you hurt someone, it makes it harder to look at yourself in the mirror. The simple thing would have been going back to the devil you know. The hardest thing is taking that first step in believing in yourself."

I think this is the most advice I've gotten from my father in a long time. "Thank you, Dad." He waves his hand as if he's dismissing me. I can't help but laugh.

"No need to thank me. Your mother is the one who raised all of you to be the best you can be. I just enforce her rules, but don't tell her that. She might start thinking she doesn't need me." Now we are both laughing. Probably because it's true.

"Seriously, though, you need to start dating again. It's not healthy for you to stay in the house every night. Stella needs to see that you are a survivor. You can be hurt, but you can love again. Otherwise, she will never dip her toes into the pond. She'll be waiting around for the right one to show up on her doorstep. You know life doesn't work like that. She's a very smart child and you will have your hands full with her."

"It's so hard for me to put myself out there."

"Why, because of your Parkinson's?" He always seems to hit the nail on the head. Making me admit things I really don't want to.

"Yeah, I don't want to be anyone's burden."

"So, then don't be. Have a plan in place so that never happens. Not just for your partner, but also for your daughter. It's time you stop playing the pity card. Now you better put the rest of the cannoli in the fridge before I eat them all." He made his point, and now he's done. Never been one to dwell on anything. He'll always give advice, but it's not always what you want to hear. I take one more cannoli out of the box before I put them away.

"Dad, I'm going home. If you need anything, call me." He waves me off and I head home. Now I have to work on a profile for a dating site. The older I get, the harder this is getting.

Chapter Ten

Fitz

When I get back to the office, Sal is gone. It's just as well; sometimes the quiet helps me get into the zone. The first thing I do after grabbing my coffee is fire up Amran's laptop. I can't help admiring how organized he was. He has folders on his desktop. Inside the folders are more folders. I find one labeled *dating*. I open that one only to find three more folders. Each one is a different dating website. When I go into one of the next folders, there are spreadsheets. If nothing else, he's making it easier for me to look into his life. It's very sad that this is what his life comes down to—a bunch of files and spreadsheets on his laptop. I pull up his photos. I'm hoping I can compare them to the dates that he had. Nothing seems out of whack. Next up, I go into his social media accounts. Everything seems normal there, too. He's a young guy that seemed to be very social. That doesn't mean he didn't hide his depression. At some point in life, we all get depressed. We all handle it differently. Unfortunately, some can't handle it at all. Nothing seems wrong. There is no blatant reason for this man to kill himself. I think I want to work backwards . . . look into the other known cases of suicide and see if something connects them. Since Gail and Captain Hart retired, it's harder for me to get the information I need. Having not one but two hackers as part owners of this business comes in handy. I won't bother Travis since he's in daddy mode right now, but Sal can help. I pull out my cell to shoot him a text.

Me: Hey, I need your skills. Where are you?

Sal: Out, but I can be there in twenty minutes.

Me: Hmm, that must mean you are with someone. Female? Date?

Sal: See you in twenty.

Well then, I guess it's safe to say there's a woman in the picture. Eventually, he'll bring her around. I wonder how Hudson will deal with it. While I wait, I dig around on social media trying to find out more about the other suicides that Father O'Neil told me about. Every one of these guys looks happy. Not that it means much. Everyone has a mask they hide behind when they need to, and I'm no exception. I decide to narrow down my search to the medical examiner who performed the autopsy on Arman, along with any of the other suicide victims, since they lived in the same area. That narrows it down to three, the same three that Father O'Neil gave me the newspaper clipping about. Justin Michaels was a lawyer. Franklin Jasper was an accountant, and Arman Blankenship was a doctor. There is something here, something I'm missing. Hmm, wait, all the profiles say "in a relationship" yet there are no names or pictures of a new boyfriend on anyone's profile or social media pages. They all joined a dating site, which, in today's world, is no big deal, but no pictures or a name—that's a flag. The door chimes and in walks Sal, finally! "I need your computer skills."

"Hello to you, too. What's your problem, now?"

"No need to get pissy. I'm sorry I interrupted your date." I'm trying not to laugh at the scowl on his face.

"For your information, it wasn't a date. I was with Hudson." Now my ears perk up. "I met her on her break. She feels bad about leaving us high and dry here. She offered to fill in when she can. I told her no. I don't need her exhausted. That's when mistakes happen."

"I totally agree with you. Hand to God, I promise not to be so picky when you are interviewing candidates." I don't push him about his personal life with her. I didn't think it was a good idea from day one that they get involved.

"Now what do you need from me?" He pulls a chair up so he can see what I'm doing. I quickly give him the lowdown on everything.

"Fitz, even if Father O'Neil is right, how could you make someone commit suicide? I get that you can murder someone and make it look like suicide, but I would like to think the medical examiner would figure it out."

"If the ME is busy and all signs point to the obvious, they might not look any further. Especially if they have no reason to." He leans back in his chair, crossing his arms, like he's waiting for more from me. "Sal, as far as getting someone to commit suicide, I would have to dig a lot deeper before I go down that road. I want to make sure I turn over every stone before I go back to Mrs. Blankenship. She deserves to know the truth, no matter what it may be."

"Move over. If nothing else, you make an excellent case." I wheel my chair out of his way. I appreciate that he's giving me some latitude on this one.

"If I think like you—which is some scary shit—your theory could work. With the same ME, I would like to think he or she would have noticed something. However, we all know there was only one Gail. She always went above and beyond. Anyway, let me tap into the ME's computer system and pull his notes from all three cases. Just because the same ME signed off on it doesn't mean he did the actual autopsy. I'm printing out everything for you, since I know you like to have it spread out in front of you. Someday you are going to have to embrace technology and stop killing so many trees."

"Thank you, I've been getting better. I'm actually learning all the things my phone can do. Especially, since it literally saved our lives on more than one occasion." I get up and head toward the printer. "So, who is this person you're interviewing tomorrow?"

"She had to reschedule because of a family obligation for next week. At least she contacted me and wasn't just a no show."

"Send me an invite, so I can put it on my calendar. I promise I'll behave." I say, while trying not to laugh. He grumbles and goes to his office. I gather everything and head into the conference room. The first thing I must do is put each autopsy report side by side in date order. I've worked on many serial killer cases. I've seen things that have kept me up at night. The one thing all killers have in common is their signature. Rarely do they vary from it. Each one of these men did not die the same way. Arman's was from a drug overdose, while Justin Michael's death was a gunshot to the right temple. Franklin Jasper leaped to his death from his Manhattan office. I look through each one's personal life. They all joined dating sites, but not all of them were the same. They were all in a relationship, however, there are no pictures or names of whom they were involved with. All of them were career men. The first thing I want to do is talk to the ME. If I leave now, I should be able to get to his office in Manhattan before he leaves, especially since I'll be going against rush hour traffic. I pull out my phone to give MJ a quick text.

Me: Hey, I'm heading into the city. I should be home about 6-ish.

MJ: Okay, I'm still at Travis's house. They came home about an hour ago. Piper is a doll.

Me: Maybe we should have another baby?

The three dots are blinking, and it seems like forever.

MJ: Trust me, that awe feeling you are experiencing right now will pass. We already have two kids to put through college.

Me: I thought it's the woman who is supposed to get these feelings?

MJ: You're a marshmallow in a Superman cape lol. Love you; be safe.

Me: Love you, too.

Marshmallow, my ass. I head out and hop on Wanda to head into the city.

Chapter Eleven

Fitz

Normally, I wouldn't take Wanda into the city. My baby means way too much to me, but I'm pressed for time. Thankfully, the drive into the city doesn't take that long. I'm able to catch the ME, a Mr. Johnson, before he's done for the day. Although, he doesn't seem happy to see me. "Hi, sir, I'm Fitz Rodriguez. I called earlier about a few of your cases." I reach out to shake his hand.

"Hi, yes, I'm just getting ready to leave. Do you mind walking while we talk? I pulled the files you were inquiring about. I don't see a problem. All three were suicides."

Now here is where I have to tread lightly. "Please understand, I'm not second-guessing your work. There seems to be a rise in suicides within the gay community. One of the mothers is questioning the death of her son. I would like to give her some closure." At this, he stops short, turns toward me. His eyes are fixed on mine.

"Mr. Rodriguez, you have a reputation that proceeds you, so I'm going to give you a little latitude here. The same as you, I don't take my job lightly. All three men died at their own hands. I understand that when this happens, it is very hard on those left behind. It will serve them best if you suggest counseling to them rather than stoking the fire with some sort of tinfoil hat conspiracy theory. Now, if there is nothing else?" He doesn't even wait for me to answer. He turns and walks away.

Yeah, I don't think so. I race after him, slamming my hand against the door before he can open it. I've backed him into the corner. I'm a big guy and he looks lost next to me. "There is no reason to be a prick about this. Like I said, I'm trying to give a family some closure instead of a cut and dry report. I'm not stoking anyone's fucking fire. I don't believe in conspiracy theories or the tinfoil brigade. What I do believe in is the God's honest truth that everyone is entitled to. Unfortunately, I have to waste my time making sure you did your fucking job or if you just signed off on it. I get that you only have the body to work with. However, I have everything else, so if I'm coming here with questions, you damn well better answer them. Now, did you do the autopsies, or did you sign off on them?" His face pales. I drop my hand and take a step closer.

"I signed off on them. Due to budget constraints, when something is obviously a suicide, the autopsy is done by a junior colleague. I review it and sign off on it. I can assure you that everything was done properly. Now, if you would please excuse me, I've got a train to catch."

Pick and choose your battles wisely. This one is not worth my time. He has nothing to offer. I step to the side and let him pass. I head outside to Wanda, and I find Hudson is sitting on her. "Hey, how'd you know where to find me?"

"You taught me some wicked tracking skills."

"So, it must be important if you felt the need to track me down." I throw my thumb up in the air to gesture for her to get off of my baby. Ignoring me, she looks down and runs her finger along Wanda's frame. I can wait till she is ready to tell me what she's obviously struggling with.

"This is hard, Fitz. I never thought it would be you I come to for advice on my love life or lack thereof."

"Well, I can understand why you would come to me. After all, I've got it figured out."

"I know I'm going to regret this, but what is it?"

"The key to happiness, kid. Now, tell me what the problem is." I take a step back and give her a little time and space to gather her thoughts.

"It's Sal. I told him I want to be friends. Not friends with benefits, just friends. I think he's pissed off and I feel guilty. He wants to know why. Hell, I don't know why. I just know that he's not my "it," as you would say." I knew this would happen. This is why you never shit where you eat.

"Do you want me to talk to him?"

"I don't know what you can tell him that I haven't already said. He's making me really uncomfortable. I've been picking up double shifts, so I don't have time to help at the agency. Which is sad because I enjoy working there. I don't want to avoid family gatherings or helping at the firm but it's uncomfortable being around him."

"Hudson, it's been uncomfortable for quite some time, so why don't we address the elephant in the room? It pissed you off. He told me you took the police exam." I put both my hands on her shoulders. "You need to understand he was scared. He had to tell someone, and he trusts me. He wasn't looking for me to jump in and stop you. No one could change your mind once you've made it up. He just didn't know how to handle everything. When you're upset and need someone to vent to, you go to your friends, right?" She gets off Wanda while pushing my hands away.

"If you remember correctly, my best friend died. That's what brought you into my world. What I have now is you and your family. They've become my family and friends. I don't want that to change and, for your information, I forgave him, although, I let him grovel for a while. It's just not there, Fitz. That "it" factor that everyone looks for."

"I'll talk to him. You don't have to worry. I will not let anything come between our family." I glance at my watch. If I leave now, I can get home in time for dinner with the kids.

"Go ahead; I know you've got to get home. My break is over anyway. I'll see you in the morning."

I pull her into a hug. "Be safe out there." I watch her as she heads up the block and gets into her squad car.

It's still rush hour, and I'm hoping I make it home in time for dinner. As I navigate Wanda through the streets, I can't shake the feeling that Hudson is holding back on me. She never does, but something is off. When I get out of the tunnel, traffic is at a standstill. This is when Wanda is at her best. I zip in and out of lanes, pissing off the drivers who can only wait and watch. It's not long before I pull up to my house. My conversation with Hudson is weighing heavily on me. I try to shake it off, taking the steps two at a time. When I get inside, Bacon runs past me, followed by Patrick and Mary. It's just another typical crazy night at the Rodriguez' house. I run behind Mary and scoop her up. Her laughter is contagious. Patrick races around the table and leaps toward me. Luckily, Mary has crawled around to my back. With her arms around my neck, she holds on tight as I catch Patrick. We fall on the floor laughing as Bacon runs up and licks Mary's feet. "How was school today?"

Mary throws both hands up in the air. "I don't go to school, Daddy." Her eyes fill with tears and her little bottom lip quivers. "Why can't I go to school?"

"You will be going soon enough. Right now, we want to keep you with us." I tickle her and her infectious laughter is back again.

Her tears are gone. I get up, taking both kids with me. "Time to wash up for dinner." We head into the bathroom. I wash up first and then leave them to finish up.

"Hey, beautiful, how was your day?" I put my arms around MJ's waist from behind and nuzzle into her neck. She always smells wonderful.

"It was good, well, except for Dad telling me we need to watch what we say around the kids. I'll tell you all about it later. Dinner is ready, so get everyone settled in, please." God only knows what the kids said. We were doing the spelling thing for a while, but nothing gets past Patrick. I'm running after the kids when Andy comes in with Stella and Jacob. He's juggling a tray of corn bread, which smells fantastic. I swipe a piece as I run past him. We get seated at the table. Both dogs are next to Mary—*gee, I wonder why.* She thinks we don't know that she sneaks them her food. We finally get settled in and tonight we tap Patrick to say grace.

"You got this buddy," Andy says while tousling his hair.

"Bless us, O' Lord, and thank you for making my mom a wonderful cook, amen."

"It was a shortened version, but it will do. Amen, now let's eat." I put a piece of corn bread on Patrick's plate and pass the rest around.

"Fitz, I stopped by the agency, but Sal said I just missed you. Does he seem off to you?" Andy asks. I glance from him to the kids and back to him. He picks up on my silent message.

"Sorry I missed you; everything okay?"

"Yeah, no big deal."

"Andy, if you've got no plans tonight, hang out after dinner, please. I've got some stuff I want to go over with you."

"I've got no plans. Besides, Stella is sleeping here tonight. The kids have no school tomorrow. I was thinking maybe we could take them for a long weekend upstate. I think the Dutchess County fair is going on." The sound of MJ's fork dropping startles us all. I'm afraid to look at her. I can feel the flaming arrows she is mentally shooting at me. When I finally find the nerve to glance up at her, her face is flushed, just as I predicted. However, it's Andy that's in her crosshairs.

"Andy, why? For God's sake, why? What would possess you to even suggest this? You know my feelings about going up there. There are plenty of fairs out on the Island that you can go to. Hell, I'd even go with you if that would make you happy." I've learned years ago that the last thing I want is to step in between a brother and sister fight.

"How about we table this for now and we can talk about it tonight. In the meantime, Andy and I will clean up since you cooked."

"Deal. Come on kids, tonight is your lucky night. Everyone is excused from the table. Get your bathing suits on. We've got one hour for some fun in the pool!" It's amazing how fast they move when it's something they want to do. Everyone is running around laughing while Andy and I watch.

"Fitz, is she ever going to let us go upstate again?"

"Not in this lifetime, my friend. She only tolerated it because we enjoyed it. She still blames herself for going into early labor with Patrick." When I close my eyes, the memories of that day come flooding back. I feel a wave of anxiety hit me in the chest. I open my eyes and quickly look away from Andy.

"Fitz, don't go down that road of guilt. I go down it enough for both of us. Remember, I was in that room when that madman shot her. I should have been able to protect them both. Unfortunately, my reflexes are no longer sharp, and it showed that day. I just thought it might help us all if we could try to replace the bad memories with some good ones."

"You know your sister. She's like a dog with a bone. I don't know, maybe she's right. Maybe we need to make fresh memories elsewhere." I get up and start clearing the table. "Come on, let's get this done, so we can get the kids outside." I shelve the conversation for now.

The kids finally wore themselves out. Andy and I helped them build a fort in the living room. They are fast asleep in their sleeping bags, with both dogs standing guard. I grab a couple of beers, thinking we can talk and head out back, only to find Andy cleaning the barbecue. "Andy, why?" I ask. MJ is giggling. I clearly stepped into the middle of something.

"Your wife fucking guilted me into it."

I pass them both a beer. "Dare I ask why?"

"Because I went on a date with Stephen. Apparently, you were more interested in making sure I was okay."

"Well, she has a point. I did burn the entire dinner because you wouldn't answer your damn phone. But forget that for now. I need your help, both of you." Andy takes a seat and MJ pulls hers closer. "It's Hudson and Sal. She came to see me today. She was upset and not sure how to handle things." I quickly fill them in on our conversation.

"I knew something was up when I stopped by the agency today. Sal is walking around like he lost his puppy. What are you going to do about it?"

"I don't know, which is why I'm asking both of you for advice. You both know I made my feelings clear from day one. I never wanted them to get involved." MJ is silent, which is odd. Usually, when it comes to stuff like this, she has some ideas. "Hey, babe, what's wrong?"

"I think there is more to this story. I know she was pissed that he talked to you about her decision to take the police test. But that's not something that can't be fixed. Let me try talking to her. You need to get more out of Sal." I'm running through everything she's saying, but then she picks up her beer and wraps her lips around the opening. She tilts her head back and slowly takes a long pull of her beer. Sweet Jesus, my cock just lost its mind. I hear Andy talking in the background, but it only sounds like that stupid noise machine that MJ swore would help the kids sleep better. All it did was drive Bacon crazy. She puts her beer down while slowly running her tongue over her lips. She knows the effect of what she's doing is having on me.

"Andy, it's time for you to go home." Her voice is throaty. I never take my eyes off her lips. He gives my shoulder a gentle squeeze, laughing before heading out the door. My eyes stay focused on her hands as she stands up, unties her bathing suit top and tosses it in my lap. She knows her breasts are my kryptonite. With the unspoken promise of enjoying them, I would move heaven and earth. There is a slight chill in the night air. When it dances around her nipples, it causes them to become hard, almost as hard as my cock. With both hands on the back of the chair, she slowly leans in far enough for me to slowly swirl my tongue around her nipple. First one and then the other before I finish off each with a little nip. She climbs into my lap and her body withers with each nip of her nipples. I'm pretty much keeping it together. That is until she lets out a cross between a moan and a low growl. When this happens, all bets are off. I'm out of the chair with her legs wrapped tightly around me until she uses her heels to push my bathing suit down. I'm still having my way with her rock-hard nipples, and in one quick move, I literally rip what's left of her bathing suit bottom to shreds. Pushing everything off the table as I slowly drive my cock home, where it belongs.

Chapter Twelve

Stephen

Seeing Andy again made me realize how much I've lost. A loss that was totally my fault. In the end, I let my fear of Andy's disease take over the rational side of my thinking. He was rocking the boat by bringing Stella into our lives, as well. I still can't wrap my mind around the fact that Andy is a dad and, by the looks of him, a very happy one at that. He talked about being someone's difference. I tried to understand what he meant. Maybe I wasn't enough. Or was it me not showing him what he clearly needed? Maybe I wasn't really his hundred percent all along. We all hold back a little, never completely baring our souls to anyone. Maybe there is too much of a divide between us to ever get back what was, what could have been. When I look over at Stone lying in my bed, I feel nothing. He wants to take it to the next level, but for me, there is no other level with him. The only one I ever had that with was Andy, and I really fucked that up. I don't want to be lonely anymore. My thought was if I committed myself to Stone, the loneliness would go away. It hasn't. It's only made me realize how empty my life is. I have everything on a silver platter, yet, without Andy, I have nothing. Maybe the person I should talk to about all of this is Fitz, that is, if he doesn't kill me the minute he lays eyes on me. Stone begins to stir, and I make no move to get back into bed. What I'm doing with him is wrong, and it makes me feel . . . I don't know, almost dirty.

"Stephen, come back to bed. I'm lonely." He reaches his arm out, waiting for me to take it.

"I can't. I've got an important case to work on. I'm going in the shower. You can let yourself out." My words sound hurtful and harsh, even to me. He's out of the bed and instantly steps behind me, wrapping his arms around my waist. I almost flinch at his touch. "Stone, I really need to get to work. Honestly, this isn't working for me. Maybe if I was younger, like you, my mindset would be different." He's not letting go, instead his grip gets tighter.

"Stephen, you know you want me, you need me. So, what's the real problem here?"

I turn around in his arms. "Stone, I wish I knew. I just know this is not it. I'm sorry," I plead. He leaves a trail of kisses down my chest. I don't want this, yet, my cock is hard, so very hard. When he drops to his knees, he swirls his tongue around the head before he effortlessly glides my cock all the way to the back of his throat. I grab a fist full of his hair with the intention of stopping him. You know that saying "The road to Hell is paved with good intentions." Well, I'm on a fucking express train right now, bound for hell. I pull at his hair as I buck my hips. He looks up at me, his eyes filled with water, no doubt because I'm slamming into the back of his throat, hard and fast. All I can do is close my eyes and pretend it's Andy. I can't help it; it's not Stone that I want. With my release, I scream Andy's name. I'm too embarrassed to look down at Stone on his knees. His hands are firmly gripped on my ass as he slowly releases my cock from his mouth.

"Who's Andy?" He gets up and tries to pull me close to him.

"Someone from my past. He is of no concern to you. I've got to get in the shower and then go to work. Please be gone when I get out." When the hell did, I become such a prick? I finally look at him and for the first time I notice a sadness about him I didn't see before. Now I feel like a first-class ass. "Stone, I'm sorry. I'm just not ready for any of this, whatever this is."

"Don't worry, Stephen, I'll be here for you when you are ready."

I quickly head into the bathroom, hoping he'll be gone when I get out.

Stone

This one is going to be harder than I thought. I knew he came out of a long-term relationship a while ago, but something is pulling him away from me. These are the ones that should be the easiest to manipulate. All the Stephens in the world fulfill my need to make them see they have no purpose in this life. They are hurting the ones they claim to love. I had him, but then something changed. While he's in the shower, I quickly go through his nightstand. If he's got something to hide, he will keep it close by, especially if it means a lot to him. Sure enough, under a few papers, I find a photo of him with another man. When I turn it over, it's dated the 24th of July 2011. Written under the date is "The day our lives began." Stephen and Andy. When I move some more of the papers around, I find a divorce decree stating that Andrew Justice and Stephen Cooper are no more. I snap a quick picture on my phone of the photograph and the divorce decree. I know I can look everything up when I get to work. One of the many advantages of being a judicial clerk for a top New York City criminal judge. Quickly, I pair my phone to his and place a few AirTags in the items he carries every day. The range is not that far, however, Stephen is a creature of habit, add to that the *Find My Friends* app, and I shouldn't really have a problem tracking him. When I hear the water turn off, I know that's my cue to get the hell out of there. Making sure I put everything back the way I found it, I grab my clothes, throwing them on as I race out the door. Now I need to find out everything I can about Andrew Justice.

It's a gloomy Monday morning, but I've made it my business to get to work early. For some reason, Monday is not the worst day for the court system, it's actually Thursday. Since I clerk in the criminal court, it doesn't matter what day it is—I'm always busy. When I want to research stuff for my own personal needs, I find it's usually best to come in very early. I clerk for the Hon. Justin Cunningham. He usually has a very busy calendar. Security is used to seeing me come in very early. However, at this hour, the research is for me and not the judge. The first thing I do is put the name Andrew Justice into the system. After what seems like forever, two files pop up: one is the divorce decree, and the other is adoption paperwork. As I read through it, I can tell the divorce papers must have been drawn up by Stephen. It has his cut-to-the-chase-no-bullshit style all over it. The adoption paperwork says nothing about Stephen, only Andrew. It does give me an address in Brooklyn. I tap into the register of deeds for Kings County and find that Andrew Justice's address is current. He owns the property outright. Before I can dig any deeper, the judge arrives earlier than usual. I quickly shut everything down and clear my browser history. The last thing I need are some prying eyes. With coffee in hand, I head into the judge's chambers. "Good morning, sir. How was your weekend?"

"It was good, Stone. Got some fishing in and took the wife antiquing. I'm sure your weekend was much more interesting," he says with a chuckle. If he only knew the truth, I'm sure he wouldn't be laughing.

"I went to the Morgan Museum. They have one of the best collections of rare books."

"I will have to tell my wife about it. I'm sure she will want to drag me there. Anyway, what's on the agenda for today?"

"It's a pretty quiet day, well, except for the appeal request for the drug lord Joaquín Escobar. His attorney is claiming jury tampering. He says one of the juror's sister's died of a drug overdose, which prejudices him."

"What's your opinion on all of this?"

Every case that comes before him, he always asks me what I think. He knows I failed my boards, yet he acts like my opinion matters. "Everyone's life in one way or another has been touched by drugs. If you eliminate them all, you will have no jury pool to pull from."

"Leave the brief on my desk and I'll get myself up to speed. Thanks, Stone." That's his way of dismissing me. No doubt his decision will reflect my answer, it always does.

Chapter Thirteen

Makenna

Life hasn't always been easy. Who am I kidding? It's been absolutely crazy from the day Andy brought Fitz home. We've been inseparable for so long, I don't know any other way. I nurture, it's what I do. My mom has enough on her plate taking care of my dad, so when Andy became sick, I jumped right in and I've never looked back. So, when he does things on his own, I worry. Let's face it, when it comes to my family, I'm the worrier. When Andy decided to meet Stephen, I thought I would lose my mind. Fitz, of course, didn't help matters any. First, he tells me he's worried and tracks him down. In the next breath, he tells me we have to let Andy live his life. I wanted to scream at him, but I know that would not get me anywhere. Instead, I decided to talk to my dad. Like me, he has a clearer head. For a hot minute, I actually thought I should talk to my mom, but when she whipped out the rosary beads, I knew that was not a good idea. The best way to get my dad to give his full attention to anything is to bring him a few cannoli from his favorite bakery. When I open the front door, I'm hit by the blaring noise from his television. As soon as he sees me, he immediately mutes the television. He glances at the box and back toward me. "You must want some advice. I have to warn you, your brother was here earlier and brought some cannoli," he says with a laugh. I pass him the box and take a seat across from him.

"Dad, I'm struggling and I'm not sure what to do. It's about Andy." He opens the box and pulls out a cannoli. He's staring at it for a bit, but then he bites into it. A smile slowly comes to his face. The taste for him is nirvana.

"While I enjoy this, why don't you tell me what's going on."

"Andy went out with Stephen." Before I can continue, he holds his hand up, stopping me.

"MJ, I know all about it. He is an adult, and you need to respect that. I know you always want to fix everything but, in this case, you can't. They have a history that, for whatever reason, is not over. All your mothering will not change that."

"But what if he gets hurt again? What about Stella and the rest of this family?"

"You are fierce when it comes to protecting him. You get mad if anyone brings his Parkinson's front and center, yet, you use it too, just in a different way. I know you are not doing it to hurt him but keeping him squirreled away so no one and nothing can hurt him is basically doing the same thing."

His words hurt even though they are not meant to. However, they still do. "How do I protect him but not smother him?" He pops the last bite of his cannoli into his mouth, taking his time to, no doubt, formulate the right words that I need to hear.

"I think you need to trust him more. He's a highly educated man that, unfortunately, also has an incurable disease. Help and guide him to make the right choices for him and his daughter. I'm not saying he needs to forget that he has it. On the contrary, he needs to make the right choices for him and Stella because of it. I told him today that he needs to put himself out there. He needs to show Stella just because someone isn't perfect doesn't mean they can't have it all. As his sister and best friend, you need to reinforce that. He doesn't need another mother, MJ, trust me; one is enough." He turns his head to look toward the kitchen, no doubt checking to see if mom is there. I know he's right but being right doesn't make it easy. If anything, it makes it harder.

"Okay, I understand what you are saying. I'm going to help him put himself out there, for him and for Stella. I'm going to support him even when I don't agree with him. If it gets really bad, I'll drag Fitz into it. Thanks, Dad. As always, you are a fountain of wisdom." Before I can say anything more, he picks up his remote and waves me off. I grab the box of cannoli and take them back to my house.

Andy

Courage . . . bravery, adventurousness, guts, determination, no matter how I spin it, I need it. But I don't have it. What I do have is fear, a lot of it. The only thing that is fueling me forward is Stella. I thought when I married Stephen, that was it. My mom always says, "it's harder to stay than it is to leave." I never really understood the gravity of her words until Stephen walked out of my life. He took the easy way out, even when I chose to stay, to try harder. I ended up coming home to an empty house. It was literally empty. Well, except for the cold-as-ice goodbye note. I'm staring at the blank computer screen when suddenly Jacob jumps up from his nap on the couch and races toward the steps. "Andy, it's me," MJ bellows as she closes the front door. At least she always announces herself before she comes in. She heads right into the kitchen and pours herself a cup of coffee.

"What's in the box?" I ask her as if I didn't already know.

"Cannoli. Do you want one?"

"Did you just come from Dad's?" I can't help but laugh out loud.

"Yeah, I figured he didn't need them, since you brought some over this morning." She curls up on the sofa next to Jacob and mindlessly pets him.

"MJ, you can always come here and talk to me. You don't even need to bring me any cannoli."

"I know. It's just that Dad gives brilliant advice, even when it's not what I want to hear. I'm sorry for trying to run your life how I think you should live it. If you feel you want to try again with Stephen, I will support you no matter how stupid I think you are."

"Somewhere in there I think is an apology, or at least as close to one as I'll ever get, so apology accepted. The thing is, I want to see what's out there, but I'm not sure where to begin. I'm older and I have an illness. Do I disclose that or do I wait? I've been out of the loop for so long, I do not know what dating sites are reputable or just hook-ups? There are a lot of unknowns here. I'm too old to make a stupid mistake."

"Andy, you are not too old. Hell, they have sites for people over sixty now. It's all about making the right choice and being the best salesman. Do you want me to help you with your profile? I'm not butting in or anything; I just want to help." She is holding her breath, waiting for my answer.

"Yes, I would love your help." She grabs the pad and pen from the end table and passes it to me.

"The easiest way to make a profile is to make a bullet list. Write five things that are a deal breaker."

"Okay, must love kids and dogs. You know, with all of us combined, we are one big, crazy family."

"So, you want to look for someone who is a family man. Do you want someone that is a business owner or someone who works out of the house? At the end of the day, Andy, the person needs to fit in with our brand of crazy."

"Well, they need to work outside of the house. I can hardly get anything done with all the interruptions. How could I expect anyone else to?" I get up and refresh our coffee while she grabs the laptop and finds a service she thinks is good.

"We will keep it short. A wonderful picture and a snappy tagline should do the trick. How about this?"

Escapism at its most romantic.

I'm a single dad who loves the family life. When I'm not teaching my daughter about life, I can be found cooking a great meal or enjoying a cold beer. I'm straightforward with a positive attitude. Oh, and you must love dogs. If you are intrigued, drop me a line.

Andy

"Wow, MJ, you are amazing. After reading that, I want to date me." She throws her head back and laughs.

"All we need is a fantastic picture, and you are on your way. Now, here is my mama bear rant. I love you, and I trust your judgement. However, you have to be careful. We can always have Fitz check someone out, if need be. I'm not paranoid, just cautious. Now, I've got to get home and you need to pick up the kids. I'll see you later." She gives me a quick hug and heads out. I can tell myself I want to be independent, that I can take care of myself, but at the end of the day, it's all about family and who has your back.

Chapter Fourteen

Fitz

When I get to the office, Sal has all three files spread out on the conference table, along with three laptops that are open. He seems to be working between all of them. I look at the clock and it's early, too early for him. "Did I miss the memo that today we were going to start at the crack of ass today?"

"Oh, I didn't hear you come in. Last night I couldn't shut my mind off. I kept trying to figure out how someone could possibly persuade someone to take their own life."

"I warned you what would happen if you got inside my head. It's a very scary place to be sometimes. What did you come up with?"

"It's too neat. Everything here is practically gift wrapped with a pretty bow on top. I know I'm missing something that is staring me right in the face, but I can't figure out what the hell it is."

I get us both a cup of coffee and sit down next to him. Each computer has the Instagram account of each victim. "What about family? What do we know?"

"The only one with any family was Arman. For one reason or another, Justin and Franklin didn't have any immediate family that I can find."

"Sal, Arman had a best friend: Matt Daniels. What can you find out about him?"

"Do you have anything more than a name?"

I dig around in the box and find the picture. "Does this help? If not, I can call Mrs. Blankenship to see if she has his contact information." He takes the picture, scans it with his phone and uploads it to the computer. Just when I think I have a handle on all my phone can do, he reminds me how little I know.

"Got it. Matthew Daniels works for The Department of Sanitation in Staten Island. Give me a minute and I can get his cell number." I don't know why I'm amazed at how quickly he can come up with so much personal information.

"Fitz, I can feel you staring at me. You shouldn't be shocked; this is what I do. We all have a talent, this is mine. Oh, and I just tracked him. He's at work." He jots down a number on a sticky note and passes it to me.

"Thanks, Sal. It's still early. Maybe I'll head to his job and surprise him." I put the number in my pocket and head out, leaving Sal combing through all their social media accounts.

Whenever I need to clear my head or think a case through, I jump on Wanda. I do some of my best thinking on my Harley. Something keeps gnawing at me. It didn't start until Sal was flipping through all the Instagram accounts. As I near the Verrazano Bridge, I'm happy that the top is open. It's a double decker and ever since I was buried alive in a building, I don't like confined spaces. Matt's work is not that far from the bridge. It's at the end of a tree lined residential neighborhood. Basically, it's an enormous garage where sanitation trucks are stored. There are a few men hanging around outside. When I tell them who I'm looking for, they direct me to the inside office, which is basically a glass booth with a desk inside. There is a guy on the phone. Before I can even knock, he's waving me in. He quickly finishes up his call and offers me his hand. "I'm Matt Daniels. The guy's out front said you were looking for me. What can I help you with?"

Interesting that they gave him a heads up so quickly. "I'm Fitz. I'm here at the request of Joan Blankenship. She asked me to look into her son Arman's death. She doesn't believe he committed suicide."

"Please, have a seat. I don't know what I can tell you." He pulls a chair out for me to sit on.

"I understand you were his best friend. Just talk to me, tell me what you think. Is it possible he did this?"

He twirls his pen, watching it spin in circles. He closes his eyes, takes a deep breath, and when he opens them, he finally looks at me. All I see is a distant, lonely stare. Finally, he clears his throat, but takes his time, almost like he is choosing his words carefully. "Arman and I have been friends since kindergarten. We were always together until he went to medical school. He had offers from so many schools, however, he chose CUNY School of Medicine in Harlem. Arman was the most non-judgmental person ever. He loved kids. 'If we give them the chance, they will change the world for the better.' That's what he always said. He believed everyone learned differently and never saw the color of their skin or their religion, only the love in their hearts. Once he graduated, he became a pediatrician and stayed in Harlem. He had no time to invest in meeting people, so he relied on dating websites. Not that there is anything wrong with them; it's a new world out there. There were a lot of relationships, but nothing that lasted. Arman's downfall: he was a workaholic and few people wanted to put up with that." He gets up and grabs two waters from the small fridge and passes me one. He stops and gets that blank stare again. I'm hoping I didn't lose him.

"Please, whenever you're ready, tell me everything you think I should know." That's it. His eyes grow wide and the grip he has on his water bottle is so tight water comes out the top. He grabs a paper towel and blots up the water.

"I agree with Mrs. Blankenship. Arman loved his life. He lived to help people. It's not feasible that he would take his own life. Plus, he was a devoted Catholic and very close to his mom. I went to talk to the medical examiner, and he basically blew me off. I read the letter and nothing in there sounded like Arman. But how do you get someone to commit suicide?"

"Did he mention any names of the people he was dating?"

"The last six months he was dating someone with an odd name, but for the life of me, I can't remember. Before I packed up his apartment, I went through everything. Honestly, there were a few things—private things I didn't think he would want to share—so I put them in a box and took them with me. The rest I brought to Mrs. Blankenship. She put everything in his room she kept at the house, as I knew she would."

At the sound of this, the hair on the back of my neck stood up. "What kind of stuff? Do you still have it?"

"Yes. My plan was to look into his death myself, but I didn't know where to start. Like I said, the medical examiner was useless." He gets up and goes to a small closet in his office. He pulls out one of those white cardboard file boxes and passes it to me. "I've kept it here because seeing it only upsets my wife, Susan. We all loved Arman."

"Do you mind if I look through it?" He shakes his head no before lifting the cover off and pushing it toward me. There is not a lot of stuff left in the box. The first thing that catches my eye is a stack of photos. I pick them up and begin to look through them. "Do you know who any of these people are?" I ask as I keep flipping them.

"No, I don't know any of them. However, most of them have names and dates on the back. There are a few journals too, but I couldn't bring myself to read them."

"Would it be okay with you if I take everything with me? I promise I will give them back to you when I'm done." He pulls a large shipping envelope out of his desk draw and passes it to me. As I gather everything, I'm reminded that this is what's left of someone's life. All their hopes and dreams are reduced to this.

"I didn't tell Mrs. Blankenship about all this his stuff. When I had some answers, I was going to give it to her. I didn't want her to have the personal journals, if they were going to cause her more pain." The sadness is back, and I feel sorry for the heavy burden he's been bearing alone.

"Thank you, Matt, for sharing this with me. As soon as I come up with anything, I will let you know." I head out to Wanda and secure everything in one of my saddlebags before heading back to Brooklyn. Everything Matt said and didn't say is weighing on my mind, but something is still bothering me. It's not a long ride back to the agency and, thankfully, Sal is still there.

"Hey, how was your meeting with Matt Daniels?"

I pass him the envelope and grab a cup of coffee before taking a seat. "It was very interesting. That is everything he held back from Arman's mother. He didn't believe the suicide and wanted to investigate it. He just didn't know how. Matt tried talking to the ME, and you know where that got him. Something is still bothering me from earlier. Did you find out anything more while I was gone?"

"You know, Fitz, I took my focus off of Arman and started really looking at the other guys. They had profiles on dating sites, however, they never crossed paths. There is something there and I just can't figure it out."

I'm looking at the screens again. *Arman, Justin, Franklin . . . drug overdose, gunshot to the head, leaped off of a high-rise . . .* Finally, what was in the back of my mind is front and center. "I got it!" I leap out of my chair, knocking it over. "It was murder, not suicide, and I can prove it! The answer lies with Justin. He was lefthanded, yet, the gunshot was to his right temple. Why the hell didn't anyone see this sooner?"

Sal's fist hits the table so hard, everything rattles. "Damn it, Fitz. I knew there was something right in front of my face, but I couldn't figure it out. At least now we have something to get the ME to take a second look for real this time."

"I think you should go talk to the ME. He doesn't like me much, and this might make him shut down. Plus, just because one is a murder doesn't mean all of them were. We need to dig deep into each man's life and see what we find. I don't want to be accused again of subscribing to a tinfoil hat conspiracy theory, as the ME called it." Sal rolls his eyes at the mention of a conspiracy theory.

"Is he still breathing, Fitz?"

"Yes, but I'm sure he is gone for the day. He keeps bankers' hours, which really makes me miss Gail. I think from this point forward, we have to investigate every suicide as a homicide until proven otherwise."

"I hate to say this, Fitz, but I think since you established some sort of relationship with the ME, you should probably be the one to bring him this new information." He shuts down the laptops before heading out.

I am looking through the photographs Matt gave me. I could spend forever going through them and still have no answers. The journals might be the best lead. I lock up the pictures and the files but take the journals with me. I figure when everyone goes to bed, I can spend some time getting to know Arman.

Chapter Fifteen

Andy

Stella had so much homework tonight, I never thought she would ever get it done. Finally, the dishes are done, and she is fast asleep. I decided I'm not going to tell her anything about dating until I find someone I can trust in my life. I love the picture MJ put up as my profile picture. It's a simple photo of me in a leather jacket sitting on the edge of the Marine Parkway Bridge. I have a thing for bridges and love to explore them. Usually, I'm with Fitz when I do, but, on this particular day, it was just MJ and me. I'm hoping I might get a few responses to my profile. I don't know why I'm nervous, but I feel butterflies in my stomach as I log on. Oh my gosh, I have one hundred and fifty-seven messages! I can't possibly go through all of them in one night. I need a beer before I start this. After heading back into the kitchen and grabbing a beer, I go back and stare at the screen like it's going to bite me or something. I click on the message box and slowly begin reading. It's amazing to me what people will say when they are not face to face with the person. Hudson always calls them keyboard gangsters. After reading some of these, I can understand what she means. It doesn't take me as long as I thought it would to dwindle them down to twenty-five men that have piqued my interest. Now I need to look a little closer into their profiles. I've learned a lot from Fitz over my lifetime. He's always had a list or rules that he follows. I probably should have been writing them down over the years. It would have made for an interesting book. Foremost is never accept anything at face value. He always says everyone has a mask they hide behind when they need to, and I'm no exception. I wish I had his gift to see through the crap. I could ask MJ for help with this, but she'll go all mama bear on me. Another hour passes and I'm no further along than I was before. I grab my phone and look at the time. It's still early for him.

Me: I need your help with something. Nothing earth-shattering, so keep it to yourself and head over when you can.

Not even five minutes goes by and I hear the key in the door. Fitz comes strolling in with a beer in hand. I try not to laugh, but I can't help myself. "I'm sure MJ told you she helped me join a dating site today. Well, I didn't think this would be so difficult. I got one hundred fifty-seven messages. I've dwindled it down to twenty-five, but that's where I hit the wall." He smiles as if the thought of me needing dating help from him strokes his ego.

"I keep telling you I'm the man. I've got the 'it' figured out. Maybe I should start an advice column." He sits down on the couch next to me and pulls the laptop toward him.

"Hmm, you need to look at some of these a little closer. Here's an example; this guy Tim, he's a typical breadcrumber."

"What the hell is that?"

"He will string you along, but never really meet up. His message is very generic. He's trying to say he has the same interests that you do, but you hardly talk about your interest in your bio. That's a breadcrumber. Next." He deletes the message and goes on to the next one. "This one might be catfishing. Looks too perfect. Once you establish a contact with anyone, you need to find them on the different social media sites. I'm sure you already know this, but never give out too much information. Here's an example: where do you live? You can say Brooklyn, but don't say Bay Ridge."

"Fitz, the way you are plowing through these, I'll be lucky if I have one date." That's when it happens: my quick look behind the mask. "Talk to me, Fitz. What is going on?"

"It's a case I'm working on. It's hitting a little too close to home for my liking. Look, you need to make me a deal. Before you go out with anyone, you will tell me first."

"Why? I mean, I'm not an idiot. I'm able to take care of myself, and I'm usually cautious when I decide."

"Hand-to-God secret, Andy, the case I'm working on has to do with gay men getting murdered, but it's made to look like a suicide. The only thing I can figure out so far is they all were on different dating sites. You picked a hell of a time to start dating again. Are you sure there is no hope for you and Stephen?"

I know when to push and when to accept what he's telling me. It must be bad if he would rather see me with Stephen. "It's that bad, Fitz?"

"It is, Andy. If I'm not around, get in touch with Sal and he can help you check anyone out."

"So, are all of these out?"

"Are there any you find really interesting?"

I narrowed it down to three. "I think I would like to meet these three." He does a screenshot and sends it to himself. In the age of modern technology, here's hoping it will keep everyone safe.

"Okay, if you don't need me anymore, I have to get back to the case I was working on. I'll get back to you later about the three of them." He gets up and heads toward the door. Suddenly, he stops and turns back around. "Andy, please be careful out there." He doesn't wait for me to answer; he's already out the door.

Fitz

Of all the times for Andy to get back into the dating scene, he had to choose now. If I told him to wait, he would, but that would be punishing him for someone else's crime. Besides, I can't even prove there was a crime yet. Before I immerse myself in Arman's journals, I decide to make a pot of coffee. Except I find MJ already did it. She left a note: *"Don't get too lost in your case. Remember, I'm here for you . . .waiting."* The one thing I don't need reminding about is how much I have. I thank God every day that I survived. I love my life and always give back when I can. That's what I want to do for Mrs. Blankenship. Give her some sort of peace. After losing a child, I don't even know if that is possible. I head into my office off the front of the house. It's the quietest room in the house, even with the bank of screens that affords me a street and backyard view. The journals are dated, so I decide to start at the beginning. Writing in a journal is very personal. No one ever expects them to be made public. These are his most intimate feelings, but I have no choice. His journals start during his senior year of high school.

> "I have finally decided to come out to my mom. With Matt's encouragement, I just told her everything I was feeling. It washed away all the fear I had inside of me when she asked me if I was happy. I took my time and thought about it. Not having to live a lie anymore . . . yes, I'm happy for now.

I say for now because I know times are changing, yet in some ways, time stands still."

I jump ahead to the time he is in college and the relationships he had back then. My thought is maybe someone from the past, a jilted lover or a professor. All the relationships he talks about are nothing out of the ordinary. He spent most of his college and med school years focusing on becoming a doctor. I finally get to the point where he has established himself as a pediatrician.

"Today I realized what led me to choose my profession. This is me making a life, not just for myself but for all the kids I help along the way. They are the future for all of us. Now, if I could just figure out how to fit in some sort of relationship with someone, my life would be complete."

There is an eight-month time gap until his next entry.

"My life has been so busy that I haven't had time to keep up with my journaling. That's a bad thing for so many reasons. Journaling helps me keep my thoughts organized. It helps me see where there is room for improvement. I'm dating someone who sits down with his cup of coffee and journals for fifteen minutes every morning. I wish I was that disciplined. His name is Jason, and he is amazing in so many ways. I used a dating app for the first time and he was my first actual date from there. I don't want to think too far ahead about

making a lifelong commitment with him. When I do that, it usually ends in disaster. He did say he wanted to talk to me tonight about something important to him. Maybe, just maybe, I could hope he wants to take it to the next level."

Jason is the first relationship mentioned so far but there is no last name or the name of the app that he used. Quickly, I jot it down for further research. There is a three-day gap before he journals again.

"I thought Jason was the one. Sadly, the big talk was him ending it with me. He wanted someone that would be more devoted to him. My job was a big contention for him. Not so much the job in of itself, but the amount of time I devoted to it and not him. I can't give up what I love just to please someone else. If I do that, in time, I will resent them. How do I find someone who can help me balance both? I guess I have to keep putting myself out there or just resign myself to the fact that I will always be alone."

Wow, my heart is breaking for him. Maybe the loneliness was just too much for him. Maybe he really did commit suicide. There is another gap in his journaling, but not as long as the first one.

"I met someone totally different from the type of man I'm usually attracted to. There is something about him that grabbed me from the first time he shook my hand. His eyes are an

amazing blue and when he looks at me, I swear he can see down to my soul. He has almost a boyish look about him with a deep clef in his chin and dimples to match. He says he is twenty-two, which is a little young for me, but I could not say no. I'm trying not to get my hopes up, but it's really hard not to."

Damn it! What the hell is his name?! I continue to the next entry hoping he says a name.

"He has a great job with the courts while he is studying for the bar exam. He knows what it means to devote your time to your profession. Plus, he has no problem with me being a doctor. I thought, wow did I really find what I've been looking for for so long? Will I be able to handle it, exclusive . . .maybe. He wants me to get off of the dating sites. All he talks about is being exclusive. Maybe he senses my appreciation. Maybe it's just his insecurity. It's like he is becoming clingy. It seems his version of exclusive and mine are totally different. I need time to process all of this."

That journal ends and I quickly find the next one. Still no name, but the signs that there is trouble between them is very obvious, well, at least to me it is. Then again, it is easy to see what the problems are when you are on the outside looking in.

"Easter service was a beautiful sunrise service, except it was just mom and me. I told her that I met someone. I try to be upbeat when I talk to her about it. My dad died in a car accident when I was a junior in high school. My mom has been alone ever since. I wish I knew why she never tried to meet anyone, but it's none of my business. Instead, I try to be the best son she could ever ask for. She finally decided to retire after years of teaching. As a gift to her, I'm going to take her on a vacation to Poland. We still have some family there, and it's something she always wanted to do. I will talk to her more when the time gets closer."

All his thoughts are apprehensive about the relationship he is in. So far, all I know is that the guy is younger than him, studying for the bar exam, and he works for the courts. He needs to give me a damn name!

"The depression is hitting me harder than it ever has. My meds don't seem to help anymore. Maybe it's just me. I find I'm turning into a needy, clingy person. The type of person I despise, but why? I'm excited I'm going to dinner with Matt and Susan. I have not seen them in months. I've been so wrapped up in work and my life with Stone that part of my life just seemed to slip away."

Finally! Stone. Matt said it was an odd name. When I reach for the phone to call him, I realize how late it is. It's something that can wait until the morning. I'm not sure if that's his real name, or some made up identity. At least I know what he does for a living. Maybe Sal can piece enough of this together to find out who this guy is. I saw nothing in the coroner's report about medication. I need to take a second look at that, too. I'm nearing the end of the journals. I want to get to the end, yet, I don't. I already know how Arman's story ends. What I don't know is why.

"Today, I asked Stone if he would come to church with me and my mom. I felt it was time I finally introduce them. He said no, he would never go with me to church. Our lifestyle goes against everything the church stands for. He said my mom would be too embarrassed if we both went to church with her. It's one thing if it's just me. They can keep whispering behind my back, but with him there, it's out in the open. How could that be? God loves me, he loves everyone. My mom has always been my biggest advocate, accepting and loving. Stone is wrong, he has to be wrong. Does he know something I don't? My mom calls here all the time. Did she speak to him when I wasn't here? I would think she would have told me. I think I need to talk to her myself and find out what is going on."

That's it. That's the last entry. He never made it to his mom's house. I'm sure a lot more transpired between these journal entries. What is here is what Arman decides to reveal. It's what was important to him. The mind games and the possible question about Arman's medication could turn this whole thing around. I put the journals away and begin flipping through the pictures, not the front but the back. The ones with names and dates on them. None of them have the name Stone. I put the ones with names back in the box and lay out the rest face up on my desk. I take out all those with women or older men, and what I'm left with are five men. Two are African American, so I eliminate them. Now I'm down to three very good-looking white men. One is only a side view, almost like the person didn't know the picture was being taken. Tomorrow, I'll bring them to Sal and see what he can find out. I make myself a note to double check on the men that Andy was looking at. You can never be too careful. Finally, I lock up the house and head upstairs. With so much on my mind, I don't think sleep will come easy.

Chapter Sixteen

Andy

After Fitz narrowed down my potential dates to five and then left me with a warning, I was too nervous to do anything. I opted to binge watch *NYPD Blue*. The series took place in Brooklyn south. It started in 1993 and ran until 2005. In the beginning, it was very gritty and realistic. Toward the end, not so much. Maybe it's like that with everything in life. It always starts on a high note, and then not so much. Anyway, it's a beautiful Saturday morning, so I'm going to put aside everything and spend the day at the park with Stella. I love spending time with my family, but some of my best days are spent with just me and Stella.

I put together a fabulous breakfast and head into her room to let her know the plans for the day. I am not saying that she is the most easygoing child ever because she is my daughter; she doesn't let life get her down. She is deaf, so life is a little different for us. Instead of knocking on her door or leaving it open, I've had alerting devices installed all over the house. With the press of a button, her bed vibrates. There are strobe lights in all the detectors in the house. Jacob is trained to alert us both if there is any danger. Those are just a few, but installing them gave Stella not only her privacy, but her chance to be like everyone else. Let's face it, that's all kids want is to fit in. Later on, they realize they should stand out and be who they want to be. Before I can alert her that breakfast is ready, she is already heading out of her bedroom.

"Good morning, Stella. How did you sleep last night?"

"Okay, I fell asleep reading my book and I can't remember where I left off."

"I hope you are hungry. I made your favorite: french toast with grilled pineapple." She makes a plate for Jacob after I put everything on the table. She has been trying to learn to speak and not just sign. It's very difficult, but she is determined to do it. Today she wants to say grace. I cannot put the pride I feel into words. Any version she chooses is fine by me.

"Bless us, Lord, for these gifts and my dad's good cooking. Amen!"

"Perfect, and thank you for liking my cooking. After breakfast, I thought we could go to the park today, unless you want to do something else?" Her cheeks turn red and she looks anywhere but at me. I tap her cheek and she turns her head back toward me. "Stella, you know you can tell me anything."

"You know how my school is having the Easter party and I'm supposed to go with Patrick? Well, Anthony Di'Mazza asked me to go with him. It's not a date, Dad, I swear it's not. I know the rule is no dating until I am sixteen. I wanted to ask Aunt MJ if she would take me shopping today so I can get something new to wear. I asked Patrick if he would be mad at me for going with Anthony and he said no, because like I said, Dad, it's not a date."

She is signing so fast, even I'm having trouble keeping up with her. "Not a date, right?"

"No, I promise, Dad."

"Well, finish breakfast and then we can go see if MJ has time today to take you. Is that fair?" She leaps into my arms, nearly knocking me out of my chair. I guess I get the good dad award today.

MJ will never say no to Stella, and today was no different. Fitz was already gone when we got there, so I stayed home with Patrick and Mary. While they watch a movie, I open my laptop with about as much courage as I had last night. The messages are back up to an insane amount again. Going through all of this is a full-time job. I'm about to start weeding through them when the motion sensor alerts me to someone by the front door to my house. Travis practically has the entire block monitored. When I open the app, I see Stephen is at my front door. "Patrick, I'll be downstairs if you need anything. I have my phone with me." I yell out to him and he waves, but his attention is on the movie they are watching. I activate the camera in the family room before I go. When I open the front door, I see Stephen sitting on my stoop. Now I'm annoyed more than anything else. "Stephen, what are you doing?" I call out to him. He sees me, and jogs across the street. "Why are you here?"

"Andy, we need to talk."

"So, you chose to sit outside my house? We already talked. I wished you well, Stephen. It's over. I don't know what else you want from me."

"This is not over for us. It will never be over. Andy, we need to find a way to make it work."

I glance at my phone to check the kids. Nothing has changed.

"Look, I have to get back upstairs. I'm watching the kids right now and it's almost lunchtime. I'm sorry, Stephen." I turn to leave, and he grabs my arm a little more forcefully than I would have expected.

"Andy, I thought about what you said and I'm ready to make you my difference in every way you need me to."

"You must do it for you, Stephen. You have to want so much more out of the relationship than you've ever given before. It's too late for us. Take care of yourself." He lets go of my arm. I turn and go back inside, locking the door behind me. As I head upstairs, I turn on the camera and watch him walk away. I know it's the right thing to do, but sometimes doing the right thing really sucks.

Stone

Some days, I have to remind myself that the world is counting on me to make everything right. After getting no answer from Stephen, I decided to do a little snooping around, which just happens to lead me to the same neighborhood that Andrew lives in. Coincidence? Yeah, I don't think so. As I take in the neighborhood, I notice all of the cameras. That's when I decide to cut through the alley to get to Andrew's block. Imagine my surprise when I see Stephen sitting on the steps of what I think must be Andrew's house. I really want to confront him, but I would have a lot of explaining to do. Stephen is far from stupid. I hear his name being called, so I stretch my head around to catch a glimpse of him. I can understand why Stephen is so not over this guy. He is sporting a tight black t-shirt and jeans to match. Damn, I can feel myself getting hard from the sight of him. The discussion looks heated, that is, until Andrew turns to leave. That's when Stephen grabs his arm. I really wish I could hear what they say. He drops his hand down and takes a step back. Andrew heads inside while Stephen is just standing there, looking very rejected. He turns and heads toward me. I quickly turn around and race out of the alley. When I get to the corner, I pull my baseball cap down low, make a left and just keep walking. If I can't get Stephen, then maybe it's time I go after Andrew.

Chapter Seventeen

Fitz

As predicted, sleep never came. When I get downstairs, I grab a cup of coffee while trying to navigate amongst the usual Sunday morning chaos. MJ is trying to make some sort of sense with Mary's hair. Patrick and Stella are playing a game of tag while Andy is standing by the window with his coffee cup tight in his hand. When I step next to him and stare out the same window, I see nothing that is of any interest other than my grass in the backyard needing to be mowed. "Surely you are not this fixated on my grass. What's wrong?"

"Just lost in my thoughts, not a big deal. If we don't leave now, we will be late for mass. You know how mom gets if we are late." He puts his cup in the sink and begins rounding up the troops. I give him his privacy for now.

Father O'Neill's message today was about judging people. Look inside yourself before you judge someone else. After reading Arman's journals, I realize this must have been what he was dealing with—the judgement of others. We always go back to Mom's house for Sunday brunch. It thrilled me that Travis, Livy, and baby Piper joined us today. I try to never work on Sunday, but this case is eating away at me. Thankful that my family understands, and everyone is too busy fawning over the baby, I'm about to head out when Travis pulls me aside.

"Fitz, I need a few minutes before you leave." He pulls out his phone and passes it to me. It's a video from the front of my house. Stephen is walking across the street from Andy's house. The video doesn't last long. Maybe this is what was eating away at Andy today? I pass it back to him, but he shakes his head no. "Keep watching, Fitz."

The video is different views from our block, the alley and 5th avenue. There is a guy with a baseball cap pulled down low. There is no view of his face. The only thing I can tell is that it's a white guy with blond hair sticking out from the cap.

"Fitz, he seems to be watching Andy and Stephen. When Stephen left, it looks like he follows him. I'm not sure what you are working on, but you need to let Andy and Stephen know. I split it into two videos if you want to leave the part with Andy out of it. If you want me to talk to Stephen, I can. You know calmer heads will prevail."

I forward the videos to my phone before giving it back to him. "I think I should talk to Andy first. Let me see what he has to say."

"Okay, is Sal helping you? If he can't, let me know and I can jump in."

"Sal is helping, so no worries, but I might swing by later to bounce some stuff off you. I don't want to pull Andy out in front of everyone. Can you let him know I'm outside and I need to talk to him, please?" While he goes to find him, I slip out front. I sit down on the top step and pull out my phone, so I can play the videos again. When I look up, Andy takes a seat next to me.

"Fitz, you could have told me yourself that you needed to talk to me. Why so cryptic?" I pass him my phone and hit play. He's very quiet while he's watching them.

"Wow, I'm so used to the cameras that most of the time I forget they are there. Stephen came by yesterday while MJ was out with Stella. He is not taking no for an answer. And before you get all caveman on me, I can and did take care of it myself. The bigger question is who the guy is with the baseball cap?"

"I figured I would ask you first before I go to Stephen."

"Why do you have to talk to him? Maybe the guy is new in the neighborhood. Not everything in life is sinister, Fitz. Oh my God, you think this has to do with the case you told me about?"

"I don't know, but I don't take chances. I'm going to go talk to Stephen." I get up and head toward Wanda. Before I start her up, I look at Andy and I see the concern for Stephen is still there, it's written all over his face. Maybe this is why Stephen keeps coming around. When I start her up, he gets up and heads back inside. I want to stop at the office first and see if Sal can do anything with the photos and the information I've gathered before I head to Stephen's. He rarely works on Sundays, but he said he wanted to get some stuff together for the person he was interviewing tomorrow morning. Sure enough, when I pull up, he's still there. I cut Wanda off, grab all the new info I have, and make my way inside.

"Hey, I'm glad you're still here. I've got some stuff to share with you from the case." I'm pulling out my notes and the pictures when I notice he's dressed up in a suit and tie. "Crap, Sal, who died?"

"No one died. I'm having an early dinner with Hudson before her shift."

Instantly, my nerves are on edge. "Did she suggest it, or did you?" It's the only thing I can think of that is somewhat nicer than what I'm really thinking.

"I told her we need to talk. It's time, Fitz, this dance around the elephant in the room is over. I want to move on. I know that's what she wants, and I figured I could just move it along faster."

"Did you meet someone?" I ask. His eyes go wide, and he has a shit grin on his face. "Damn I'm good."

"Shut up and tell me what you need."

I quickly fill him in and share the videos with him. "While you work on this stuff, I'm going to talk to Stephen."

He scans the photos and gives them back to me. "What if that guy has nothing to do with any of this? Have you thought about what you are going to say?"

"No, I just have a bad feeling that this is somehow connected. I'll just fly by the seat of my pants on this one. Good luck with Hudson." I laugh as I race out the door.

Things were easier when Stephen lived across the street. Now, on a good day, it's at least forty-five minutes to his midtown co-op. I probably should have called first, but sometimes the element of surprise is a good thing. Besides, the doorman has to ring him, so that is enough of a notice. Surprisingly, he sends me right up. This is the first time I'm seeing Stephen since the day he walked out. There has always been a tension between us, but after I retired, I was around more, which made it worse. He never liked what I do but understood why I felt I had to. I have to help those who can't help themselves. MJ jokingly calls it my Superman complex. She's not that far off the mark. No one helped my mom when my dad beat her to death. She locked me in the bathroom to protect me. Andy's dad rescued me. He saved my life, and I will always be grateful for the life he gave me.

When the elevator doors open, he is standing there. He looks thin and somewhat sad.

"Fitz, what brings you to my doorstep?"

I step out of the elevator. "Can we talk inside?" He waves his hand toward the door, and I head inside.

"I was just getting myself a beer. Can I get you one?"

"No, thank you. I'm driving. I came here because I'm working on a case and it might involve you."

"I can't image that I could be a part of anything in your world. Please, have a seat."

The way he says *my world* grates on my nerves. He leads me toward an area that looks like it came out of a high-end catalog. As I look around, all I can think of is Mary and how she would come in here like a wrecking ball. I clear my head and I pull out the photos first. "Stephen, this is personal, but I need to ask, anyway. Are you on any dating websites?"

"You're right. It's personal and none of your business. Why do you need to know?"

"It seems someone might be killing off gay men on dating websites," I inform him. He shifts in his seat, but his eyes never leave mine.

"How is that even possible? What kind of proof do you have? Why haven't I heard about this before?"

I spread the photos out on the coffee table. "Do you know any of these men?" He picks them up one at a time. The last one is the photo that only has a side view of the man. He takes a little longer look while running his thumb over the photo before he puts it back on the table.

"I don't know any of them. Is that it? That's not proof, Fitz. You would get laughed out of court with that so-called proof. Why is this not in the news or at least being talked about in the gay community?"

"Actually, I have two videos for you to watch." Travis split them into two videos so I could hold back the one of him and Andy. I don't want him to think he is getting the better of us, most of all Andy. I pull out my phone, put it down in front of him and hit play. The first one is of him and Andy. The second one is the man with the cap. "What went on between you and Andy is your business. However, don't hurt him, Stephen. Do you think the guy in the cap was following you? Have you seen him before?" I know I need to mind my business when it comes to Andy and Stephen's so-called relationship, but It's a sore spot for me.

"I honestly do not know. How did you even get these videos? What do you have the entire neighborhood wired?" A look of disgust flashes over his face.

"Just about. In today's world, you can't be too careful. So, you have no idea who any of these men are?" I wave my hand over them again, but his eyes don't come off of the video of him and Andy. "Stephen, the reason this is not being talked about is that they are classified as suicides. After digging into each case more, I've come to realize that at least one or two of them were not suicides."

"Andy and I met the other day, which I know you are aware of. I talked to him about getting back together. When he left, I took what he said to heart. I showed up at his house yesterday to talk about it, but he wants no part of me. He won't even listen to anything I have to say. He says it's over. I say it's far from over. Don't look so shocked, I will not get all stalker on him. But when I think about it, Fitz, I know I fucked up royally. I was scared. I mean, he was throwing a kid with a disability into our lives without even talking to me about it. I panicked and ran. I'm not proud of my actions, but I'm human. I apologized but, apparently, that's not enough."

"I've never known you to be so judgmental, Stephen. She is deaf and more capable than people with no disabilities. No wonder your apology is not enough. Who made you judge and jury?"

"Andy did when he made me fall in love with him and then got sick. He gave me an out before the wedding. I stayed and put everything I had into taking care of him and your family while you were out playing cops and robbers."

"You can blame me for whatever you want. I have always appreciated how you took care of my family, but you can't blame Andy for getting Parkinson's, for Christ's sake. That's insane! What you don't get is that when you used Andy's disease against him, you broke his heart. He gave you his heart, and you stomped all over it. Now you come crawling back, thinking he would take you back with open arms?! Listen to yourself, Stephen, you are talking about his child like she is a burden when, in reality, she has more compassion and kindness that you could only wish to possess. Do you think my family would forgive and forget what you did? And for your information, I wasn't playing cops and robbers. I was protecting this city against cold-blooded killers. Stephen, let me remind you—at the end of the day—you reap what you sow." I grab everything and walk out before I say anything more that can't be taken back.

Chapter Eighteen

Sal

While the new facial recognition program is downloading, I use that time to set up everything for the interview. We've interviewed many people, most of them men. Recently, I got to assist on a case with another agency. Their case crossed over to one of ours. We worked with the owners of the agency—two women. After that, I realized that's what's missing here. We need a woman investigator. I think I shied away from hiring one because I didn't want Hudson to think she was easy to replace. My computer chimes, letting me know the program is ready. I load all three pictures that Fitz gave me. I also made a still from one of the video frames. The first two come up right away. I've got names and addresses, so that will be easy to look into that. The one with the side view and the still come up as the same person, but there is no match anywhere else. If this is the killer, then why is he looking at Andy and Stephen? I email Fitz all the information and send the unknown guy's information to Travis. Maybe his connections at the

FBI can find out something. If I don't leave now, I'm going to be late. The last thing I want to do is piss off Hudson.

We decided to meet at Ben's Kosher Delicatessen. It's a favorite for both of us. When I get there, she's already seated. "I'm sorry. I didn't think I was late." I pull out the chair and have a seat.

"You're not. I was a few minutes early and, since it was starting to get busy, I grabbed a table. I ordered our usual double dip, if that's okay?"

"That's fine. I'm going to jump right in here. We are two people who became very comfortable, very quickly. We run in the same circles, and I don't want our relationship to make either of us uncomfortable. You've told me that you've already moved on, and I get it. All I really want is for us to get to the place where we were before: grabbing a meal and having a few laughs. Are we good?"

"Wow, did you rehearse that before you came?" She smiles and it seems like forever since I've seen that.

"Of course, I did. You wouldn't have it any other way. Now, on to business. I'm interviewing someone tomorrow that is an excellent candidate to take your place." The waitress picks the right moment to put our food down.

"Okay, tell me all about her and leave nothing out." She leans in closer, as if she is going to miss something.

"How do you know it's a she?"

"It is written all over your face. Well, that and Fitz told me the last one was a limp dick, so I figured it had to be a woman."

I nearly choke on my soup. "Fitz should not be allowed anywhere near human resources or public relations. Yes, it's a woman. Her name is Gia Milano. She lives off 18th Ave and 86th Street. Her parents are from Italy. She is a first generation American with a degree in criminal justice. She is currently working on her master's but swears it won't get in the way. I did a preliminary zoom meeting with her and I think she might be a good fit. Someone who won't be intimidated by Fitz." Now it's her who nearly chokes on her soup. Finally, the laughter and the ease that we always had seems to be coming back around, and I couldn't be happier.

"Well, I have some news to share with you. I took the detective exam and passed. I didn't want to say anything until I got my results back. I didn't want to jinx it."

"Congratulations! What happens now?"

"I have to wait for an opening, but at least I'm on the list."

"I'm happy for you. I know I gave you a hard time when you started out, but you seem happy and that's all I can ask for in life."

She reaches across the table and squeezes my hand. "Thanks for meeting me, Sal. My shift starts in forty-five minutes, so I need to go." She reaches for the check, but I swipe it before her.

"This one is on me. When you get your promotion, you can pick up the next one."

She kisses me on the cheek and heads out.

Stephen

To say it shocked me to see Fitz on my doorstep today is an understatement. I wonder if Andy knows that the entire block is wired up. This is another reason why his crazy family and their lifestyle just gets in the way. Fitz lives on the edge and his family goes along with his brand of crazy. Although, if you talk to him, he thinks he is living a simple life. There is nothing simple about it. The picture he showed me of the man with a side view could be Stone, but I wasn't sure. Then the video of the guy, again, was not the clearest. Besides that, I've never said anything to Stone about Andy. I've kept that part of my life to myself. I can't imagine that he was stalking around the neighborhood. Anyway, Stone is not a killer. He would have no reason to kill anyone. He is a very good-looking, professional man, who can have any man he wants. He doesn't need to kill. The question now is, should I say something to Stone? The more I think about it, the more I think I will not say anything. Andy always said the more you know, the more involved you are. I don't need to get mixed up in anyone's drama, especially Fitz. I told Stone I have a trial to prep for, so I couldn't get together with him tonight. However, after Fitz's visit, Stone is all I can think about. I decide to text him and see if he wants to grab a bite to eat.

> **Me:** Hey, I know it's last minute, but I decided to take a break and grab something to eat at Ole & Steen. Do you want to meet me there in 30 minutes?
>
> **Stone:** I'm sorry but when you said you couldn't get together today, I made other plans. Maybe we can get together when your trial is over?
>
> **Me:** Sure, no problem.

I know I told him it wasn't working for me, but for some reason, I'm still disappointed. Maybe in my mind I'm trying to figure out if what Fitz is peddling is true. Maybe Stone has heard something. He's the one who is on top of everything that is going on. At first, I thought it was my job that keeps me out of the loop, but I realize Stone was just as busy as me. Maybe it's the age difference? When he reads the New York Post, he knows everyone in the gossip column. If I'm lucky, maybe I know ten percent. While I'm sitting here letting my mind wander, I put in an order for delivery. Something is bugging me about the video that Fitz had. If that was Stone, he would have had to follow me or maybe, somehow, he found out about Andy. I have a few things from mine and Andy's time together in my nightstand. I'm a very organized person, and I'd like to think if someone went through my stuff, I would know about it. While I wait for the food to be delivered, I head into my bedroom and open my nightstand drawer. I'm staring at the contents in disbelief. The photo of Andy and me on our wedding day is face down. Why? What would possess him to go through my stuff? If I were ready to share that part of my life with him, I would have done it on my own. The buzzer sounds, letting me know my food is on the way up. I slam the drawer and head into the living room. When I open the door, Stone is standing there with my food. I take a deep breath and slowly exhale. "Wow, this is a surprise. How did you get my food? I thought you had other plans?"

"I intercepted the delivery guy before he came into the building. I told him I wanted to surprise you for your birthday. I know it's not your birthday, but that was the only way I could get him to give me the food. Well, that and a very large tip. Surprise!"

I'm a little taken aback. I want to confront him about going through my dresser. I'm thinking it's probably a bigger deal for me than it is for him. However, he needs to respect my privacy. Just as I'm about to open my mouth, everything Fitz told me comes rushing back. What if there really is a killer? What if Stone is the killer? Damn you, Fitz! "It's a very nice surprise, Stone, and I'm sure there is enough here for the two of us. Why don't you have a seat in the living room, and I'll plate it up for us." I usually order extra so there is more than enough food. I grab two beers along with our food and head into the living room.

"Wow, you really did order enough food for two. I hope you weren't expecting company, Stephen?"

"No, I wasn't expecting anyone. I was going to review my files for my case tomorrow."

"Stephen, are you okay? You seem a little . . . I don't know—off."

I take a sip of my beer, hoping it calms my nerves. "I always worry before a trial. It took almost two weeks just to get a jury in place. Let's forget about that. Here is to tonight. I'll worry about the case tomorrow." I hold up my bottle and clink it against his. Now I need to keep my wits about myself until he leaves.

Chapter Nineteen

Fitz

Another Monday morning and my house is mass confusion, as usual. Getting the kids up, fed, and out the door for school is a lot. Starting this week, Mary is going to preschool at the church two days a week. We wanted to wait, but every time Patrick and Stella go to school, Mary cries. When she told my mom that she doesn't go to school because the school doesn't want her, that's where we draw the line.

"Fitz, you are staring into space by the coffeepot; snap out of it. What's on your agenda for today?" MJ is right. I need to snap out of it.

"I have to be at the office this morning for the interview Sal scheduled. After that, I have some leads on the case I'm working on. As always, I will try to be home for dinner. What do you have going on?" She becomes quiet, and that usually means she's got something on her mind. I pour her a fresh cup of coffee and wait.

"Fitz, I'm worried about Mary going to preschool. She's already way ahead for her age. I'm worried. I know I shouldn't be, but I can't help it."

"Babe, if you are looking toward me for some divine intervention, I got nothing. You know me better than anyone, and you know I would rather lock them in a bubble for the rest of their lives. When Mom told me what she said, it broke my heart. I rather her be a little bit wiser in years than feeling like she was unwanted."

"I know you're right. It will take me a bit to get used to it. On another note, Andy asked me to pick up the kids today because he has a coffee date. I'm excited for him, even if he's nervous."

I feel my heart pounding in my chest. "When did he decide this?" I ask while trying not to show any emotion.

"He told me this morning when he picked the kids up for school. He said you helped him narrow the list down. Is everything okay?"

"I'm sure he will be fine. Let's not take away his man card just yet." I check my watch and realize the interview will be starting in five minutes. "I've got to run, or I'll be late. Call me when you pick up Mary, so I can talk to her." I kiss her and run out the door. What I really want to do is go across the street and find out from Andy whom he is meeting. I gain my self-control as I cut through the alley to get to the office. When I get inside, I hear Sal talking to someone. Damn it, I'm late. They step out of the conference room and catch me at my desk.

"Gia Milano, this is Fitzgerald Rodriguez, one of the partners."

I extend my hand and she's got quite the grip. "Nice to meet you, Gia. You can call me Fitz. Sal and I are usually here a lot. Travis's wife Livy just had a baby, so most of his work is from home. There is one more partner, Lucas O'Brian, however, he is hardly here. The job comprises a lot of research, and sometimes you'll have to do some field work with one of us. It's not dangerous, but there can be some crazy hours."

"I only live fifteen minutes from here, but it seems parking is a nightmare. I spent forty-five minutes looking for a spot and it's not even an alternate side of the street parking day. Do you have any suggestions?"

"Actually, would you feel comfortable taking car service and we can reimburse you?"

"That's fine, but what do you do with your car?"

"Travis and I have Harley's, and no one bothers us. Most of the time we walk, since we live around the corner. Sal is a little bit further, but he gets here very early and fights for a spot." Sal seems a little quiet. For what reason, I have no idea.

"If it's slow, can I work on my schoolwork?"

"Of course, Gia. You will find that we are very laid back here. Everyone is like family."

"Speaking of which, Fitz, here comes your brother-in-law." The door opens and Andy comes in. I quickly introduce him to Gia before he pulls me into the conference room and closes the door.

"Andy, I was in the middle of interviewing her to take Hudson's place."

"Please, Fitz, she's got the job. It's written all over Sal's face. I need your help."

"MJ told me you have a coffee date. How did you narrow it down?" I pull out a chair and sit down. He follows suit.

"Fitz, I decided to message back one of the three men you narrowed it down to. The thing is, I have no clue what to talk about, nothing. It's been so long. How do people do this?"

"Calm down and show me who you are meeting." While he is opening the app on his phone, I fire up the laptop. He shows me a picture of Jordan Basile. He looks nice enough. I take the phone and use the new face recognition software that Sal got. The results are immediate. I turn the computer toward him. "Look, nothing too earth shattering, Andy. A couple of parking tickets, that's it." I'm watching him closer than usual. When he gets nervous, he begins to shake. He is clasping his hands, trying to mask it.

"What am I going to talk to him about? Should I tell him about my Parkinson's? Whose bright idea was all this, anyway?"

"Andy, focus on me, not the picture on the screen. Just go be yourself and if you feel comfortable enough to tell him, then do so. Otherwise, shut up, have your coffee, and leave. It's not like you are solving world peace; it's just a damn cup of coffee. Where are you meeting him?"

"Clockface Coffee. I figured it was close, but not too close. Fitz, what if he asks me what I do for a living? If I tell him I'm on disability, then that's as good as saying what's wrong."

"Tell him you had a business that you sold and now you're enjoying this time raising your daughter." Damn, I'm good.

"You make it sound so easy."

"That's because it is. Remember to keep your phone on and if you need an out, send me a text. Now, are we good here?"

He gets up and seems to be less rattled. "Yes, I think so, thank you. I'll let you know how I make out." He shouts back at me as he heads out the door. When I get back to my desk, Sal is sitting there staring into nothing.

"What's the problem? If it's Gia, I think she is great. If she sucks, I can fire her." He turns toward me and does a little shake of his head.

"Fitz, I gave Gia the job. I think she will be great."

"So then, what's your problem?"

"I just got the craziest phone call that crosses into your case. You better pull up a chair for this one. I met this girl. Her name is Kayleigh Barrett. We've gone on a few dates, and I like her. She is a wedding planner. That's actually how I met her. I was at a friend's wedding, and she was there, anyway I digress. She called to ask me for some advice. Her office is right next door to Franklin Jasper CPA, our dead CPA. She said she was at work when he jumped. I asked her if anyone was in his office with him and she said he was alone. Franklin moved his favorite chair and his computer into her office while his was being painted. Now that he's gone, she doesn't know what to do with his stuff. Also, she said there are men coming and going at all hours of the day and night. To her, they don't look like cops, more like people you would see in gangster movies. I kid you not, those were her exact words. She wants to know if she should do something or stay out of it and what to do with Franklin's stuff."

"Sal, you're dating a wedding planner?"

"After all that and that's what you want to know about?! Come on, Fitz, what are the odds?"

"Slim to none. Get her on the phone and let her know we are on our way over. Tell her not to talk to anyone. Give me your keys. I'll drive while you call her." He tosses me his keys and we are racing out the door.

Chapter Twenty

Fitz

The entire ride, I'm processing everything Sal said. Why am I stuck on him not telling me that he is dating someone? "Are you embarrassed to bring someone new around us? I say *us* because we are one big happy family."

"Honestly, I thought I would wait a little bit and slowly introduce her to the rest of the crew."

"Wait, you said the rest of the crew. Who else did she meet?"

His face turns beet red as he tries to look anywhere but at me. "Okay, look, Fitz, don't get mad. It wasn't intentional at all. We were dropping my mom off at bingo. You know her and your mom play bingo together. Well, she met your mom."

"My mom!" I shout as my hand slams on the steering wheel.

"Fitz, don't get nuts; it just happened. You are making a big deal out of nothing. Let's just put all that aside and focus on Franklin."

"Fine. *My mother*, of all people. What have you found out about

Franklin?" Damn, straight before this day is over, I'll be making a beeline to my mom's house to find out everything.

"He wasn't married or in any long-term relationship. Franklin was from Indiana and graduated from the University of Notre Dame. He had no living family. He was just very nondescript. It's actually very sad. What would drive someone to jump to their death? I would say let's ask the police if he had anything else they could share with us, but they ruled it a suicide."

"Which, you know, means they did nothing. Did your friend say if she knew how long before the office is rented out?"

"I didn't ask her, but I know those offices are mini condos that are owned, not leased. I didn't know that Franklin had the office next door. She said she will meet us downstairs."

When we pull up to the building, a beautiful blonde is waiting outside for us. I think it's safe to say that's Kayleigh Barrett. When she sees him, she smiles, and her face seems to light up. I put the car in park and cut off the engine before we both get out to greet her.

"Kayleigh, this is my partner, Fitz. Why don't we go upstairs and you can walk us through everything." He quickly kisses her cheek and puts his arm around her waist as he leads her inside. I quickly follow close behind.

"So, Kayleigh, how long have you and Franklin been neighbors?"

"We've been neighbors for two years. He kept to himself a lot. When everything happened, I felt so bad, like I should have reached out or something. I'm a one-person business, so I'm usually knee deep in everything. Recently, there have been so many people coming and going. Like I told Sal, not to stereotype, but they could be right out of gangster movies."

The elevator doors open, and Kayleigh and Sal lead the way. I look around the hallway before we head into her office, but there is no one around. The first thing I notice is that the walls are thin. I mean, I can hear someone in the next office flushing the damn toilet. "Do you know how many men are next door now?"

"No, I'm sorry. I'm really caught up in a wedding that is supposed to happen at The Oculus. I've got the permit and made all the arrangements, but now the bride's mother is trying to change things around, which can mess up the permit. Needless to say, I haven't been paying attention to much of anything else."

"Okay, well, just pretend I'm not here and go about your business. Sal, I'm going to try to see what's going on next door. Why don't you try to get into his computer since I'm sure it's password protected." I head to the door and open it enough to stick my head out. I can see Franklin's door to my right. I don't see anyone, so I venture out a little bit further. I'm almost to Franklin's door when I hear muffled voices. I quickly go back to Kayleigh's office. She's still busy with whatever it is she does. Sal is sitting in Franklin's chair, which is a pretty beat up, brown, pleather recliner while working on Franklin's computer. "Did you get in?"

"People think they are making up the best passwords when in reality they are so common. Fighting Irish and the year he graduated. Got it on the first try. There are numerous folders for each of his clients, but you are not going to believe who he was keeping the books for. Don't bother guessing; he kept the books for Carmine Puccio's grandson Sergio. I'm not an accountant, but even to a layperson, something is off."

"Kayleigh, are you sure no one was around when he jumped?" I ask her again, given the new information we have.

"As sure as I can be. I mean, the odd thing is his stuff is in here, so it's not like he was working on work stuff. I don't mean to be rude, but I've got to meet the bride and try to get everything worked out. Here is a spare key, just lock up when you are done." She gives Sal a quick kiss and waves as she runs out the door.

"Sal, is she always so trusting?" I wanted to add *and bubbly*, but I thought the better of it.

"Yeah, the little bit I know her, she is that trusting. I downloaded everything on his computer to my thumb drive. You have had dealings with Carmine Puccio in the past. Did Sergio take over the old man's business when he died?"

"Sergio's mother is Carmine's daughter, Angela. Her husband died in a car wreck. He was drinking and driving. Carmine made Angela move back home, and he helped raise Sergio. Carmine never wanted Sergio in the business. He wanted him to go to college and become a doctor. Unfortunately, Sergio doesn't have the brains for that."

"I think we should pay Sergio a visit. This time, Fitz, I'm driving."

"Before we go, Sal, I have one question. Why the beat-up recliner? I mean, I get that it's his favorite, but it's got to be a pain in the ass to move it. He could have covered it with a sheet if he was that worried about it."

I go over and sit in it. Sal moves the table so I can put my feet up. "This has got to be the most uncomfortable chair I've ever sat in." I get up but leave the footrest up. "Help me flip this chair."

It's very heavy, which is also strange. When we finally get it flipped over, the underneath is all stitched up. I pull out my pocketknife and start to cut away at the stitching. We are now staring at bags of money. Sal starts pulling them out, and it's never ending. We also find a ledger along with a will. Sal is trying to get a count on how many bags there are and about how much is in each bag.

"How much do you think is here?"

"Fitz, there are twenty-two bags. Each bag is marked fifty thousand. That's over a million dollars that he had hidden in a frigging chair!"

"Well, I guess that explains why he was adamant about putting the chair in here. It also explains why the men have been coming and going. They are looking for all of this. If they think Kayleigh knows anything, she can be in danger. What about the will and the ledger?"

Sal opens up the ledger and begins flipping through it. That's when a letter falls out. I pick it up and open it.

Kaleigh

If you are reading this letter, then I'm dead. This means you found everything else. I'm sorry to put the burden on you to handle my estate, but I have no one else. You were always so kind and trusting. My estate—that makes me laugh every time I think of where I came from to where I am today. Everything is pretty much spelled out for you. I have two charities that will benefit from the money you found. The reason I picked them is because of the children. They are the future. If they don't have a way out of the poverty they live in, then the world will never change. The funds were stolen from the Puccio family. They created so much evil in the world that I felt it's only right that the money goes to help those that can make a new start. Unfortunately, I got involved with Sergio Puccio. He was a great lover, but I did not know who he was. I started borrowing money from him that he freely offered to pay off my student loans. I was new in town and just starting out, and it seemed like an ideal situation. He made me need him in so many ways. Finally, when I was in too deep, he showed his hand. He used me to take care of his books. I had to find ways to launder his money for him. While I was doing that, I skimmed some off the top. Finally, one day, he realized what I was doing. He threatened to kill me, so I saved him the trouble. After you distribute the money, destroy everything, or if you are so inclined, turn it over to the FBI.

Your Friend

Franklin

"The ledger is a list of the actual accounts that Franklin skimmed the money off of. As far as the will, he left half the money to the Boys and Girls Club. The other half is left to The Bowery Mission, a soup kitchen, and a homeless shelter. Fitz, what are we going to do with all this stuff? We can't leave it here like this, and I need to find Kayleigh."

"I've got a plan."

"Awe, damn, Fitz, that's never good."

"Kayleigh has a stack of grocery bags by the door. Let's get everything loaded up so we can bring it down to the car. She said there was a problem with the wedding she was doing at the Oculus. We will head over there and try to find her. Once we have her, we will bring this stuff to the office and lock it up." He doesn't question me, which is good because, right now, I'm questioning myself.

Chapter Twenty-One

Andy

I'M LATE. I'M NEVER LATE. NOT THE GREAT FIRST IMPRESSION I planned on making. When I get inside, the place is crowded. The barista Joey makes me my usual latte as I begin to look around. Finally, I spot Jason at the back of the shop. *It's now or never, Andy.* When I walk over to his table, he smiles and stands up quickly, pulling a chair out for me. "Thank you, Jason, I'm Andy, but you know that already." I quickly sit down trying not to spill my coffee.

"Andy, I'm nervous, too. Tell me about you. What makes you happy?"

"What makes me happy is being the best dad I can be. I'm seeing the world all over again through her eyes and it's amazing. What about you? Do you have children?"

"No. I'm open to the idea of having a family, but it never seemed to be in the cards for me. What do you do for a living?"

"I had a business that I sold and now I'm enjoying my time with my daughter. What do you do? It was pretty vague when I read your profile."

"I work for an escort service. That's why I keep my profile pretty vague. I'd understand if you wanted to leave."

"Can I at least finish my coffee and ask you a few questions?" He throws his head back and laughs at this.

"You can ask. I can't say that I will answer all of them."

"My first question is very obvious. Why?"

"Money, and lots of it. I know I'm good-looking and women who are at the top of their game have no time to invest in dating. They need arm candy for certain events, that's when they call me."

"What if they want more? Is that part of the package?" He runs his finger around the rim of his coffee cup. As I watch it go around, it becomes mesmerizing.

"If they are willing to pay, I have no problem with that." His voice holds a bitter note.

"So, for lack of a better word, you're a hustler. How would you fit a family in all of this?"

He looks at his watch and pushes his chair back from the table. "This was interesting, Andy, however, it would never work out." He gets up and walks out the door. I've been on dates before Stephen and even a few after him. This has by far been the worst. That is, if you can even call it a date.

Fitz

Good luck trying to find anyone in the Oculus. It's by the Freedom Tower and is loaded with tourists all day long. There are so many, my head is spinning. Finally, Sal spots her and we slowly head toward her. I reach for Sal's arm and hold him back. "We don't want to make a scene. Let's wait until she finishes with her client."

"Fitz, we at least need her to acknowledge us." He walks into her line of sight. When she sees him, she raises an eyebrow questioningly.

"While you wait for her, I'm going to look around." I've never been to the Oculus before. I just couldn't bring myself to come back here. The vast emotions from that day . . . I've always kept buried. The Oculus is supposed to represent a white dove leaving a child's hands. I still can't bring myself to visit the 9/11 Memorial. Lost in my thoughts, I didn't realize Sal was calling out my name. "Sorry, I was just . . ." my voice trails off. I know he gets it.

"Fitz, Kayleigh is finishing up with her client. I was thinking about the situation, and I don't think she can work out of her office right now. What about putting her in the spare office where we keep the files?"

"I don't have a problem with it. You're sure that's what you want to do?" I would never tell him what to do. He has to come to that conclusion on his own.

"Why do you say it like it's a curse or something?"

"You'll need to make sure that she understands this is for her safety, otherwise, she could take it like you are moving things along rather quickly." Before I can say anything more, Kayleigh is headed our way.

"Hey, guys, I wasn't expecting you to show up here. Is everything okay?" A look of concern flashes over her face.

"Let's get to the car and we can explain everything to you on the way to my office." Sal slips his hand in hers and guides her along. I'm going to let him do the explaining. I'd rather take a back seat to all of this and watch her reaction.

"Sal, why don't I drive while you bring Kayleigh up to speed." He reluctantly hands me his keys, along with a wicked death look. He's not fond of anyone driving his car, least of all me. They both get into the back seat. While they get situated, I tilt the rear-view mirror so I can watch her reaction. I know Sal wants to believe she knows nothing about what Franklin was doing. He has more trust in the human race than I do. By the time he gets to the part about the money in the chair, her mouth is hanging open. She's either a great actress or totally clueless. I venture to say the latter. He still hasn't told her about the letter Franklin left her. When we get to the office, the parking gods are with us and there is a spot in front of the door. She gets out of the car, stops and looks around as all the color fades from her cheeks.

While Sal is getting the shopping bags out of the trunk, I lean in close to her and block his view. "Kayleigh, I know this is not your mid-town high-rise showy place that you are used to. Instead, you are getting a neighborhood filled with all different types of people from all walks of life. People that will have your back no matter what. While Sal is opening up his business and his life to you, while protecting you I might add, don't look down on him or any of us." I don't wait for an answer, instead I go help Sal with the bags.

"Fitz, is everything okay?"

"It will be. You might want to explain to her why we read the letter that was addressed to her. After you get her situated, we can go see Sergio."

We are barely in the door and the phone rings. "Sal, when is Gia starting?" I yell out as I try to grab the phone.

"Tomorrow! I'm hoping one of us can be here, so she is not by herself on her first day."

I didn't make it to the phone in time, and now my cell is ringing. It's Andy. I'm sure he wants to fill me in on his date. "Hey, Andy, hold on a sec. Sal, I'm taking this in the conference room while you help Kayleigh." I shout to Sal as I close the door behind me. "Okay, Andy, you have my undivided attention. What happened?"

"Oh, it was only one of the worst dates I've ever been on, if you even want to call it that."

"Don't tell me you thought you would hit it out of the park on your first try?"

"Of course not, but I thought it would last more than fifteen minutes!"

Oh, no, this sounds really bad. "That might be a record for a bad date." I'm trying so hard not to laugh.

"It's not funny, Fitz. You want to guess what he does for a living? Don't bother; you'll never guess. He's a fucking escort!"

Now I can't control my laughter. "Andy, that is definitely one for the record books. Look, you tried one date and fell off the horse. Get back on and try again. I'll come by tonight and we can go through the new hits you got. I'll have Sal put that facial recognition program on my iPad. I hate to cut you off, but I've got a lead I've got to follow up." When I hang up, all I can picture is Andy's face when the guy told him what he does for a living. After a quick check to make sure the Chief Medical Examiner, Mr. Johnston, is at work today, I head out of the conference room to see if Sal got Kayleigh settled in. What I find is a very frustrated Sal and Kayleigh as she's trying to explain to him why none of this is going to work.

"Hey, time out, both of you! What seems to be the problem here?" I shout out to both of them.

"Kayleigh has appointments that she needs to get to. I can't run all over town trying to keep her safe. I need her to stay here while we go see Sergio."

I'm looking back and forth between the two of them, and I know one is going to be just as stubborn as the other. "Solution: I'm on my way to pay the medical examiner a visit. After that, I will swing by and have a chat with Sergio. Sal, before you leave here, can you put that new program you have on my iPad, please?" I don't have time to waste on anyone.

Chapter Twenty-Two

Stone

The good thing about Brooklyn is the anonymity one can have being amongst so many people. Seen, yet, not seen. I knew for the right price Jason would help me. We planned to meet at the bodega close to the 77th Street subway stop. There are cameras everywhere, but I've tried to keep my face out of the camera view by always making sure I keep my cap pulled down low. As I turn the corner, I see him leaning against the wall, messing with his phone.

"Jason, you should pay attention and not always be screwing around with your phone," I snap. He locks his phone and finally puts his attention where it belongs—on me.

"Stone, you worry too much. I never come to Brooklyn, so no one knows me here."

"What happened with Andy?"

"I don't know why you are so hot for this guy. He's a lonely, gay, single dad. I gave him fifteen minutes of my time that I'll never get back."

"Did he say anything about his past?" I swear it's like pulling teeth to get anything out of him.

"No, all he said was he's a single dad and the vibe I got was that's all he cares about. Now, where's my C-Note?" I pull the money out of my pocket and slap it into his hand. "Pleasure doing business with you. I have a train to catch. Good luck with that one." He gives me the old "see ya" salute before turning on his heels and walking away. He disappears down the subway steps, blending in with the rest of the commuters. To think I left work early for this; absolutely nothing useful.

Why is Stephen so hung up on this guy? Jason was of little help to me. I need to find out more about him. Maybe what I should focus on is the kid. I'll make sure I get to work early tomorrow, so I have no interruptions while I dig into the life of Andy Justice. In the meantime, I'm going to surprise Stephen with a home-cooked meal and some mind-blowing sex.

Fitz

Today has been a roller coaster day. I mean, what are the odds that Sal's new girlfriend would tie into my case? I don't believe in coincidence. There has to be a logical explanation. I called the ME's office and gave Mr. Johnston a heads up I was coming. Just as predicted, he is waiting for me with a scowl on his face. I extend my hand as a symbol that I will play nice today with others. He looks at it and then back up at me before he crosses his arms. A typical sign that he is closed off to anything I have to say. "Thank you for seeing me on such short notice. I thought I should bring you up to speed on what I've found out so far. Franklin Jasper's death really was a suicide. However, Justin Michael's death was not by his own hand. The man was lefthanded, but the gunshot was to his right temple. I checked with his co-workers and his family. They confirmed that he was indeed left-handed. As I'm sure you know from your vast experience, it is very unlikely that someone would shoot themselves with their non-dominate hand."

"Other than which hand he used, you really have no clear-cut evidence to change the cause of death. What about Arman Blankenship? Have you found out any facts that are not wishful thinking?"

I take a slow, steady breath, so I don't throat punch this guy. "I'm not done with my investigation. If you won't rule Justin Michael's death as a homicide, then can you at least change it to undetermined?"

"I'll change it to undetermined for now, however, don't come back and waste my time unless you have cold, hard facts, understood?"

"Got it." I hurry the hell out of there before he changes his mind. I don't know Sergio's address, but I know his private club in the Ozone Park section of Queens. When I was on the force, I had dealings with his grandfather. We had an understanding that worked for both of us. He was very old school in his thinking. He didn't allow drugs in the family. For him, it was all about gambling. He loved the ponies, and we could always find him at Aqueduct Racetrack. When the old man died, he requested that the funeral procession do a drive by the track. I can't help but laugh. He probably wanted to see one last race before they buried him. When I pull up to Sergio's usual hang-out, there are four want-to-be gangsters or, as we affectionately call them, wannabe's outside like they are guarding the Pope. I park Wanda and slowly walk over. I don't want a fight, but I won't be pushed around by the likes of these goons. Of course, the biggest guy, who has no neck and probably hasn't seen his dick in years, heads right for me.

"I'm here to see Sergio. It's strictly business, and I want no trouble."

"The old man might have been soft when it came to you, but he's gone. Sergio has no business with cops. Get back on your bike and head out of here while you can still walk."

"First of all, I'm retired. Second, something Sergio has been looking for just happened to fall into my lap. Now imagine how you're going to explain to your boss that you let it slip through your hands. Finally, I have no time for your bullshit. You had your chance. I'll turn it over to the Feds. Have a good night." I turn and start to walk away, but the hair on the back of my neck stands up. I know this is far from over.

"Wait, what the fuck do you have?"

I get on Wanda as no-neck heads toward me. I open my jacket enough so he can see my Glock. "That is between Sergio and me. He knows who I am, so tell him to get in touch with me. He's got twenty-four hours." I start her up and take off. I'm not waiting around to see if Sergio wants to grace me with his presence. Eventually, I will make a deal. I'll give him the ledger, turn the money over to the charities and, to keep the peace, I won't turn the thumb drive over to the Feds. If it was Carmine, he would jump at the deal. He was all about peace. Sergio is a hothead and I'm sure he's going to fight me over the money. When I pull up to the agency, my cell rings. Caller ID says blocked. I bet I know who that is. I wonder how much trouble no-neck got into. "This is Fitz."

"I understand from my men that you are in possession of something that belongs to me."

"Sergio, my time is valuable. I won't waste it again on you. I'll meet you tomorrow morning at the 69th street pier. Let's say ten am in front of the Veterans Memorial."

"And if I don't show?"

"Oh, you'll show." I hit end before I have to listen to any more of his bullshit. The place is empty when I go inside. I grab my iPad, so I can help Andy, and head home. I leave a note for Sal letting him know I'm meeting Sergio in the morning and my agreement with the ME. Even after everything that went on today, I'll be able to make it home in time to have dinner with the kids. First, I need to stop and pick up flowers for Mary. It was her first day of school and I didn't get to talk to her. That upsets me more than anything else that went on today. Family . . . that's really all we have.

Chapter Twenty-Three

Andy

As if today couldn't possibly get any worse, I come home to find Stella in tears. Jacob is lying on the pillow next to her, licking her tear-stained cheeks, while MJ is trying to comfort her. When I look at MJ, she shakes her head no. I quietly back out of the room and MJ soon follows.

"What the hell is going on?"

"Andy, I'm going to start this by saying kids can be cruel, sometimes more so than adults. Anthony Di'Mazza told Stella his parents won't allow him to take her to the dance. On top of that, he's not allowed to play with her anymore."

"Jesus H. Christ, MJ, what happened?"

"His parents told him that you are a 'divorced homosexual,' and that goes against everything they believe in. They also told him that your illness prevents you from being a real father. You'll probably die soon and probably go to hell."

I slump on to the sofa with tears in my eyes. "MJ, how do I combat such ignorance?"

"Well, there's more. Apparently, this happened during lunch time. Patrick heard what he said and when Stella started to cry, he punched Anthony in the face. He knocked out the kid's two front teeth. He told Anthony that he was the one going to hell and not his Uncle Andy. Patrick got suspended for fighting. He made sure to tell me that he didn't say the word hell. He spelled it out so he wouldn't get into trouble."

"Well, I always knew Patrick would protect Stella no matter what. How do I handle this, MJ?"

"Oh, wait, there's more. Father O'Neil told Patrick that he had to apologize to Anthony before he can come back to school, and Patrick refused. He told Father. O'Neil and I quote, 'He made my cousin cry. God is proud of me for protecting Stella.' Andy, I do not know what we are supposed to do."

"Where is Patrick now?"

"I dropped him and Mary off at Mom and Dad's house. I wanted the time alone with Stella to understand how she is feeling."

"Besides hurt, what else did you figure out?"

"She didn't know what homosexual meant. You just always told her that you are gay and she asked me to explain what divorce meant. She also asked if you were going to die like her mother did? She said if you go to hell, then you won't see her mommy and daddy. That about killed me, Andy."

"What did you tell her?"

She sits on the sofa next to me and squeezes my hand. "I told her that homosexual was the same as gay. As far as everything else, I told her you would speak to her when you got home."

"What are we going to do about Patrick?"

"I'm going to let Fitz know what happened and see how he wants to handle it."

"You're serious? Do you not remember what he did to Johnny Fazzio for making fun of your hair?! You and I both know exactly what he's going to say."

"Trust me, Andy, I was only five years old, but I will never forget what he did to Johnny Fazzio. That was the day I fell in love with Fitz."

"When you dropped the kids off, did you tell Mom and Dad what happened?"

"I didn't have to; Mary told them they had to stay there since Patrick got suspended. You know your niece; she just blurts out whatever she wants. I can't fault her. I mean, she's only three."

I'm staring at MJ like somewhere in all of this mess there has to be an answer. I'm just not sure what that is. "I told Stella I was sick, but I have it under control. I mean, how do I explain Parkinson's to a kid when there are times I don't understand it myself?" MJ's phone rings and when I look at the time, I realize its dinnertime. I'm sure it must be Fitz wondering where everyone is.

"Okay, Dad, we will be right there."

"Dad said he wants all of us at the house now. I'll text Fitz while you get Stella. I'll meet you over there, Andy. It will be okay. I promise you, we will work it all out."

I give her a quick hug and head into Stella's room. "Hey, beautiful, I heard from MJ what happened today. I'm sorry you had to go through all of that."

"Why are Anthony's parents so mean?"

"They are not mean. This is what happens when people don't take the time to learn about other people." She pulls me into a tight hug. I never want to let her go. But she pulls back and starts to sign very quickly.

"Are you going to die like my mommy?" She sinks her teeth into her bottom lip to stop it from trembling.

"Remember what you learned in catechism? Everyone dies, Stella. God is in our lives to protect us and, if we are kind and live a good life, someday we will all be together again in heaven." This seems to calm her down. "Grandpa wants us all to come over. Why don't we see what he has to say about all of this?" She agrees. And with that, we make our way over to my parents' house. It's only around the corner, but Fitz is already waiting outside for us, holding a bouquet of daisies.

I point to the flowers. "Are you in the doghouse?"

"They are for Mary. I wanted to talk to her after her first day of school, but my case got in the way. MJ brought me up to speed on everything. Stella, I promise you everything will be okay. Let's get inside."

When we get upstairs, the TV isn't on. That's a surefire sign that something big is about to go down. Dad opens his arms and Stella runs into them. Finally, he taps her nose and points to his lips. He is the one that taught her how to read lips. He always talks slow for her and she smiles.

"I heard what happened at school today, and not just Mary Elizabeth's version. I called Father. O'Neil and got his version. After that, I called Anthony Di'Mazza's parents. Stella, when Anthony told you everything, what did you think?"

"I thought he was saying bad things about my daddy. I didn't understand why."

"Patrick, when you heard what he said, and you saw Stella cry, what did you think?"

Patrick stands up tall and proud. "I thought he wasn't being very nice. When Stella started to cry, I told him to take it back. He said no and that my whole family was going to h-e-l-l." I love how he won't say hell, but some of the other stuff that comes out of the kid's mouth is cringe worthy.

"So, what did you do?"

"I made him cry like he made Stella cry. I punched him in the face."

"Patrick, instead of making him cry, maybe you should have tried to make him understand that all people are different. God tells us we should love all people. See past them and look into their hearts for the goodness inside of them. Do you think you should apologize to Anthony? Think real hard about this, son. Remember, hate only brings more hate." Damn, my Dad is good. I can only hope to be half the man he is.

"Will he apologize to Stella?"

"Patrick, we can't make other people do the right thing. We can only show them through the good works we do and hope it rubs off on them."

"Okay, I'll go to school tomorrow and apologize to Anthony."

"And?"

"And to Father. O'Neil, as well, for causing a fight in school."

"And?"

"Oh, and to God for punching Anthony in the face, even though he deserved it."

"It's all settled. Now, let's eat our pizza before it gets cold." Dad states, slapping his knee for emphasis.

Fitz scoops up Mary, twirls her around and gives her the flowers.

"Daddy, they are beautiful."

"They are not as beautiful as you. How was school today?"

"Sister Ellen said everyone was happy that I came. Can I go back again?"

"Yes, you can. Now let's eat."

While Fitz is busy dishing out the pizza, I get Dad a couple of slices and bring them to him. "I need advice on how to deal with what was said today. I talked to her about death, and I think she gets that, but how do I deal with such ignorance?"

"Do you remember when you came to me and told me you were gay?"

"Yeah, I was so nervous, but Fitz kept pushing me too finally do it." He gets a smile on his face, no doubt remembering Fitz hiding in the doorway.

"I told you it didn't matter to me. I warned you that the path you were on would not be easy. Well, this is one of those times. I'm sure you've met with people that didn't understand how you could love another man. You dealt with them, and you will deal with this. You can try talking to them, but I have to say, after talking to them myself, I doubt you'll be able to make them understand. Or you can move forward, pray for them, and live the best life you can. When everything happened with Fitz's father, he wrote him off for dead. When the prison called and said that he was in a fight and probably wouldn't make it through the night, he came to me wondering what he should do. Would I be upset if he went to see him? I told him that was his father and I'm thankful to him for the son he ultimately gave me. You can forgive someone, Andy, but it doesn't mean you keep that person in your circle of friends. If God can forgive, then why can't you?"

"I knew Fitz's dad died, but why didn't I know that he was considering seeing him? Did he go see his dad?"

"That's not for me to say. Now, how about you get us some beers." Just like that, he is done, and I have a better understanding of what to do.

Chapter Twenty-Four

Stephen

TODAY I PRESENTED MY OPENING STATEMENT. I HAVE A strong case with a lot of solid evidence, yet, I'm always nervous when it first starts. I watch every face in that jury as if I could read their minds. I never used to do criminal law, however, when a serial killer's wife ended up being a junior partner at our firm, that all changed. Fitz might not be my brother-in-law anymore, but I learned a lot from him about reading people. My case is about the rape of Janel, a thirteen-year-old girl, by four boys who needed to gang-rape someone for their initiation into the gang. This will be a very emotional trial. I have to make sure I'm on my game at all times. The hardest part will be trying to avoid everything and staying in the zone. It's times like this I miss Andy the most. He would make sure I had a home-cooked meal. He would go overboard trying to keep me calm and focused. All I come home to now is an empty house. Hell, I don't even have a goldfish for fear I'd kill it. Walking away from Andy really made me a selfish bastard.

By the time I got home, I was starving and since I gave Stone the rest of the dinner last night, I need to go get some food. What I really want is a good burger and the best place to get one is P.J. Clark's. I always get The Cadillac with double smoked country bacon, American cheese, tomato, lettuce, and onion. Pickles on the side and fries well-done. When I get there, it's crowded, but I'm able to snag a seat at the bar. John the bartender knows me, and he quickly puts my order in, then gets me a beer. Everything that Fitz said to me has been weighing on my conscience. I wish I could make him understand how scared and hurt I was. I wonder what Andy told his parents. Was I made out to be the devil in sheep's clothing? I've come to realize that without Andy, I can't move on. I couldn't even do it when he told me about the Parkinson's. Yeah, I left. I was pissed off and hurt, but in my heart, my mind, my everything, I thought he would come for me, but he never did. Hell, I had to learn about everything that happened with him and the kid on the news. I guess I was too closed off and I admit it; I shut down. *Oh, Andy, how I wish you would walk through that door and give me a second chance. A chance to prove how much I still love you.* My food comes along with another beer. To say it's amazing is an understatement. I learned from Andy how to appreciate food and not just how it looks. I'm halfway done with my food when I see Stone walk in. What are the odds that he would just come here on his own? Am I becoming paranoid like Fitz? No matter how mad Fitz makes me, and believe you me—he can really piss you off, he usually has some valid points.

"Hey Stephen, I wasn't expecting to see you here tonight. How was court today?"

"Court went as expected. I didn't know you come here, well, at least I've never seen you here before. There are no tables, but I can move down if you want to sit at the bar." He quickly snags a bar stool next to me and places an order.

"Actually, I've never been here. A co-worker told me about it. Apparently, they have the best burgers around, and judging by what's left of yours, I think it's safe to say it's probably true." He throws his head back and laughs.

When I turn on my bar stool, I get a good side view of his face. In my mind, I snap a photograph of him. "I need to use the men's room." I get up and as I head toward the back, I can practically feel his eyes following me every inch of the way. In my mind, I'm comparing his side profile to the one in the picture. Could it be the same person? My lawyer's brain is telling me there is not enough evidence to even suggest it. However, the other part of my brain, the sexual partner of the man sitting at the bar, thinks anything is possible. When I get back to my spot at the bar, John informs me that my friend took care of the check. There is a fresh beer waiting for me.

"Thank you, Stone. That was nice, but unnecessary. I can't stay. I have court in the morning."

"At least stay and finish your beer." He pulls the bar stool out for me.

"Just this one, and then I really have to get home."

"Alone?"

"Yes, alone. I still have to review my notes for tomorrow." I take a few sips of my beer, but my mind is not focused on him or anything he is saying. There is only one person on my mind, and that is Andy. "Stone, I'm sorry, like I said earlier, I have to prep for tomorrow. I really have to go. I'll call you." I don't wait for an answer. After getting up, I slip on my jacket and head out the door. I don't even look back to see if he is going to follow me. I know now that he was nothing to me but a good fuck for a lonely man. Seeing Andy was like ripping a scab off of an old wound. I need to see this through to the end. I hail a cab and head home alone. I know it's for the best.

Stone

The bartender comes over and I push Stephen's beer toward him. "He's not coming back."

"Sorry, man, can I get you anything else?"

For a hot minute, I look at this man and think he might be a pleasurable distraction. I'm staring at him for which must seem like a long time. He holds up his hand and points to his wedding band. "I saw it, but it means nothing."

"It does to me." He walks away and at that point, I'm done. I toss some cash on the bar and walk out. In Stephen's mind, this might be over, but it's not by a long shot. Tonight, Stephen showed his hand. I'm nothing to him, nothing but a good fuck. He is just like the rest of them. Taking what he needs and then kicking me to the curb. I thought Stephen was different. My father was right. In the end, these men are all the same.

Chapter Twenty-Five

Andy

When Stella and I get home, she heads right to her room to start her evening routine. I go directly to my room to find something very important to go along with my decision to talk to her about her mom. It's a conversation that has been a long time coming. When her mom Effy died, she gave Fitz a letter to give to her daughter. We never read it, instead I decided to wait until I felt she was emotionally ready. With all the questions about my death and the mention of her mom, I feel it might be time. When I get into Stella's room, I find her asleep. Maybe this is God's way of say let her continue to be a child. There is plenty of time for all of this later. I pull the covers up and kiss her before I go into the living room, only to find Fitz sitting there having a bourbon.

"I promised you I would come by tonight. Sal was able to put the program on my iPad. I wasn't sure if you wanted to talk or work on the dating stuff."

"I was going to talk to Stella about her mom and maybe give her the letter she left her, but she fell asleep."

"Andy, maybe you should wait until she is a little older before you give her the letter."

I pour myself a bourbon and sit across from him. "You're probably right. Dad was amazing tonight. I can only hope to be half the father that he is. Did you talk to Patrick about everything?"

"It's hard for me, especially when I think the kid did the right thing. I taught him to always look after Stella and Mary. I guess, in his mind, that's what he was doing. On the other hand, I can't have him disrespecting Father. O'Neil or anyone, for that matter."

After swirling my bourbon around in my glass for what seems like forever, I take a sip and welcome the burn. "Fitz, I came to a decision tonight. I'm not sure you or anyone else is going to understand it. Hell, at times I don't even understand it. I've decided I'm going to talk to Stephen about the letter he left. Why he walked away and never looked back. Most of all, why he is now trying to come back into my life? I'm going to table the dating thing until I get all of this settled, otherwise, I will never move forward." He's looking at me like he's waiting for the other shoe to fall, except there is no other shoe.

"I'm glad you are shelving the dating thing, but not for the reasons you think. As far as Stephen is concerned, I understand you need answers, but don't be surprised if you don't get them or if they aren't the ones you are looking for."

"I went to see Stephen, just as I told you I would. He claimed he didn't know anyone in the pictures or video I showed him. He lingered on the photo of the guy with the cap, the same guy I think is in the video. If it was the old Stephen, I would think nothing of it, but after all that happened, I don't know what to believe anymore."

"Is that it? Or is there more? You might as well get it off of your chest now." For once he's in the hot seat and it feels good that it's not me.

"I might have told him off a bit. Okay, well, more than a bit. He pissed me off, Andy. He looks down on Stella and made it sound like he was doing so much for the family while I was out playing cops and robbers. Yes, Andy, that's exactly what he called it. Look, if you really feel you want to give him another chance, I can't stop you. If you decide to do that, then maybe you should both go to counseling."

"Oh, Fitz, you are really putting the cart before the horse here. I have a lot to think about, but I also have a lot of questions that I never got to ask. It's my time to do that now. Afterwards, if I want to move on, I should be able to do so with a clear conscience." He knows he is off the hook and seems to finally relax.

"Let me ask you something, Andy. What makes you think it's a good time to show Stella the letter? She is young, and we don't know what's in it. What if it's too much for her to handle?"

"What if it's not? What if it helps her move forward? This is what I'm talking about, Fitz. So many questions and the people that can answer them are becoming fewer and fewer."

"Maybe you should read it? I mean, you are her father, and you have her best interests at heart."

"I've been on the fence about it. Maybe I should talk to Dad. I mean, look at the way he handled everything today. Hell, the way he's handled everything our whole lives. Fitz, I need to ask you something. Do you remember that day we made a blood oath to tell each other everything, no matter what? Why didn't you tell me about your dad?"

He gets up and pours himself another bourbon. "When did you find out?"

"Tonight. I don't know the entire story. Dad said it was up to you to tell me. I don't understand why you didn't."

"I was ashamed. Ashamed of who he was. Ashamed of what he did and, most of all, I was ashamed of myself for not saving my mom. I had so much hate and rage built up inside of me with no place to put it. I think that's why I could do my job as well as I did because I got into their minds, but they never got into mine. When the prison called, I was glad it would be over, but I felt so guilty for feeling such anger toward him. I didn't know what to do, so that's when I went to Dad to ask him his opinion. He talked about forgiveness and letting go of the hurt and the guilt. In the end, I went to see him. I never wanted to sit and wonder what if. I realized he couldn't hurt me anymore. He couldn't hurt anyone. I told him I would not hold on to such anger because of him anymore. I forgave him and as I walked out, he died."

"I would have gone with you . . . supported you through it all. I've always been here for you, and I always will be. You know, blood oath and all."

"I know that but, honestly, it was something I needed to do on my own. Remember, I always told you, we deal with the cards we've been dealt. Whatever you decide to do about Stella and the letter, I will support you. On that note, I'm also going to let you decide what you want to do about Stephen. Maybe you are right; maybe there are more questions than answers. Just take your time. By the looks of things, I don't think he is going anywhere. Just my opinion." He laughs before he throws back the rest of his drink, gets up, and waves goodbye.

Chapter Twenty-Six

Fitz

I WANTED TO BE AT WORK TODAY BEFORE GIA GETS THERE. Unfortunately, it's never easy getting out the door. When I get there, Sal, Gia, and Kayleigh are all waiting. "Sorry I'm late. Long story short: Patrick got suspended yesterday. He knocked some ignorant kid's two front teeth out for making Stella cry. I had to coach Patrick on what his apology should sound like. When I asked him if he thought about what he should say, I got 'Dad, I got this. I'm sorry I knocked your teeth out, even though you deserved it.'" The ladies are laughing.

"Fitz, maybe you should be there when he delivers his apology, you know, just to make sure. While you are there, you can give Father. O'Neil an update on the case. Gia is going to shadow me today, and Kayleigh has some appointments."

"Sal, I can't. I have that meeting I told you about at ten. I'm going to have to trust that my son will have great follow-through. After my meeting, I'll probably stop by the church and get an update. Let's go in the conference room so I can bring you up to speed on everything." I'm not subtle, I never claimed to be. He follows me in and closes the door.

"What is it you don't want anyone to know?"

"When I meet Sergio, I'm going to give him the journal with the understanding that I will always have a copy of everything locked up someplace safe. I'll be donating the money to the two charities. The problem is, I don't think the charities will take the money knowing where it came from. Do you have any suggestions?"

"Last night I looked through the accounts again and everything filters through a dummy corporation. So, as far as anyone is concerned, the money is clean. Tell Sergio his next accountant can use it as a write-off."

"What about Kayleigh? Did you figure anything out?" He gets the stupid look all men get when they are hot for someone, even me.

"Honestly, I believe she really did not know what Franklin was doing. She is hardly in her office, which is why I think Franklin didn't have a problem leaving everything there. When you talk to Sergio, you need to make sure she is kept out of all of this. How are you going to explain it to him?"

"I will see how the meeting goes. Hopefully, I won't have to bring her up. I don't think she should go back there. You know . . . out of sight, out of mind. She can have a real estate agent sell it for her. You and I can box up all her stuff and move her wherever she wants to go. I don't think our spare office is the right place. If things don't work out with the two of you, it will be bad. If things work out with the two of you, it will be too much togetherness." That is about as tactful as I can be.

"I agree with you. I'm going to talk to her and see where she thinks she might want to move her business to."

"I have a great idea. She should move near the Flat Iron Building."

"Why there?"

"I've had to watch *Say Yes to The Dress* with MJ and Hudson. That place Kleinfeld is in Chelsea. She can get a lot of business from them." He's hysterical laughing.

"Sometimes, Fitz, I can't believe the things that come out of your mouth. I'll pass along your suggestion."

"I've got to go. I will touch base with you later." As I head out the door, I can still hear him laughing.

Stephen

I barely made it home last night. I was afraid I would fall asleep in the damn cab. This is not like me at all. I wanted to review my notes for court today, but that never happened. I almost didn't make it here on time. Right now, getting distracted would be the worst thing for me and my client. When I finish this case, I think I'm going to take some much-needed vacation. Maybe I can work on having a relationship again with Andy? First and foremost, I have to get rid of Stone. I was kind of freaked out last night when he showed up at P.J. Clarks. It's not near where he lives. Add to that Fitz's visit and I think I might be seeing a monster around every turn. I have to stop overthinking all of this and focus on my case. From now until it's over, I'm not going anywhere.

As I sit here and listen to the defense try to paint the four boys as good kids who would never do what they are accused of, it takes all of me not to lose it. The rape and the beating they gave my victim was so bad that she had to have reconstructive surgery on her face. They shoved a pipe up her rectum, then pulled it out and bashed her skull in with it. Janel is thirteen years old and, honestly, I do not know how she survived the beatings and multiple rapes. The amazing thing is she not only survived, but she is adamant about testifying. If there was ever a victim that wanted her day in court, it's Janel. I'm determined I'm going to get it for her. The prosecutor didn't want the case. He said there is not enough evidence. They wore condoms, so there was no DNA. That's when I stepped in and filed a civil lawsuit against all four boys and their parents. It's common for the gangs to try to intimidate the witness. It's illegal, but good luck proving it. So, before this trial started, I put Janel and her parents in protective custody. I'm not leaving anything to chance.

We are nearing the end of the day. I'm going to wait and have Janel testify tomorrow morning. The judge calls the day over and as I pack up my stuff, the defense attorney steps over to my table. I've been up against Susan Brenner before. She's a formidable adversary.

"Susan, what can I do for you?"

"Look, Stephen, you are out of your mind if you think these parents can come up with ten million dollars, plus your fee. What about a deal?"

"The victim—oh, I'm sorry—the plaintiff is taking the stand first thing tomorrow morning. Not only is she going to go into great detail as to what was done to her, she's also going to explain what's on the road ahead of her. Five million, I wave my fee and all four turn themselves into the police with a solid confession." Even though I know she won't take it, I still have to present it, as does she.

"I'll let you know what they decide." She turns and leaves. Now I need to go home and prepare for tomorrow. I think I'll have Jennifer Probe, a junior partner at my firm, sit second chair for me tomorrow. Just in case things get out of hand, I'll have a woman to step in. I forward her the case file and let her know to meet me tomorrow morning at eight a.m. before court, so I can bring her up to speed.

Fitz

I really hate doing business with the mob, but sometimes it's out of my hands. This is, by far, the easiest and safest way to handle this. I park Wanda off to the side, so I'm not blocking the monument. This pier is one of my favorite places to be. It's where I taught MJ how to fish, and now she's better at it than I am. I made a lot of fond memories here. I snap out of memory lane when I see Sergio's town car pull up. Those who get the furthest in his business are the ones that keep life simple. Sergio is not one of them. He gets out and heads toward me with four no-neck goons behind him. I really want to ask them if they can even find their dicks, but I think I better table that for another day.

"Hello, Sergio."

"Let me just say you were a friend to my grandfather but, as far as I'm concerned, you have no clout with me. Now, where is it?"

I open one of the saddlebags on Wanda and pull out the journal. "Here you go. The ledger of all your accounts."

"Where's the money?!" He's very agitated.

"See, here's the thing about the money. Your accountant, Franklin, he gave it to two charities. There is nothing left. Oh, except for the thumb drive with all the information on it that I have locked up someplace safe. No need to worry, Sergio. You see, as long as everyone that is near and dear to me is safe, that drive will never see the light of day. Your grandfather Carmine was a fair man. He loved his ponies, but he always kept his word. I respected him and we got along great. I'm not turning over the thumb drive to the Feds, not because of you, but because of Carmine. The way I look at it, today is a win for everyone, especially the two charities your money helped." I get on Wanda and start her up. Sergio steps in front of her and puts his hand on the handlebar. For that alone, I could shoot him.

"Someday, Fitz, I'll have something on you, and I can guarantee you I don't forgive and I don't forget."

He lets go and backs up. I've been threatened many times in my life, but I know to take his threat seriously. I take off, leaving him and the goon squad long behind me. I should just make it to the school for lunch time. That's where this mess with Patrick started. I know I'm supposed to let my kids handle their own mistakes, but I can at least be there for moral support. Besides, I need to update Father. O'Neil on the case.

When I get to the school, I go directly to the cafeteria. I hear a lot of yelling. There is yet another fight, and that's when I notice my son's distinctive shocking red hair in the middle of it. I race over and pull the boys apart. Patrick has a bloody lip and the other boy's eye is already bruising. I've got one kid in each hand when Father. O'Neil steps in.

"Fitz, I can't say I'm surprised to see you here. What is going on?"

"Let's ask them, Father, I just got here and broke it up. Patrick spill; what happened?"

"Dad, I did just like we talked about. I told Anthony I was sorry for hitting him, but before I could finish, he said Uncle Andy is a faggot. Dad, I don't know what that is, but it didn't sound good, so I punched him in the face—again." Before I can say anything, Father. O'Neil orders both boys to go to his office.

"Fitz, I'm sorry about all of this. I've tried talking to Anthony's parents, but they are very closed-minded. There has to be a way for these boys to work this out. There is zero tolerance for fighting in my school."

"Let's head to your office and maybe we can figure something out." We make our way to his office and out of earshot of everyone.

"Okay, have you made any headway on the case?"

"That's why I'm here. I can say for certain Franklin Jasper committed suicide. I'm almost certain that Justin Michaels did not. He was murdered. As far as Arman is concerned, there is no smoking gun. Unless I can find some hard evidence, the cause of death might not change. Don't give up hope, yet. I'm not done with my investigation, so let's keep praying." When we get to his office, Sister Ellen has each boy standing in separate corners of the room, facing the wall. Andy and I were in the same position many times in our lives. Maybe if I talk to Anthony, it will help. I'm about to suggest it, but that's when I see that flaming red mane come flying through the door. I don't know what's redder, her hair or her face.

"Patrick Fitzgerald, what would possess you to do the same thing today that you got into trouble for yesterday?!" I don't think she even realizes I'm in the same room. He turns around to face his mother, and she gasps at all the blood on his white shirt, as well as the biggest fat lip I've ever seen. She turns back around, and that's when she realizes I'm in the room.

"You? What are you doing here?"

"I came to see how he made out with his apology and to update Father. O'Neil on my case. Apparently, the apology didn't go so well. Before you go off halfcocked, please keep in mind this was not his fault." The words are barely out of my mouth when Anthony's parents come storming through the door.

"Father. O'Neil, would it be okay if MJ and I talk to Anthony's parents in another room away from the boys?"

"That would be a great idea. You know the way, Fitz."

We head into the inner office, and I decide I'm going to do the talking. MJ is way too upset and when she finds out why the fight happened, she will go off the rails.

"Mr. And Mrs. Di'Mazza, I want to say that I did not bring my boy up to use his fist at any given moment. However, your son has said some very troubling things. When Patrick tried to apologize today to Anthony, he called my brother-in-law a faggot. We do not put up with any kind of derogatory slur words—ever. If you are that ignorant and vile, maybe this is not the place for you." Mrs. Di'Mazza retreats behind her husband as he comes way too close to me for my liking. He's not as big as the no-neck guys I dealt with earlier, but he's big enough.

"You will not run me out of my parish just because you think that lifestyle is okay. If anything, Father. O'Neil should make you and your family leave. There is no room here for your kind of thinking."

"Your kind of thinking only breeds hate." I can feel my entire body get stiff.

MJ steps closer to me. "Fitz, they are not worth it. At the end of the day, they have to answer for their actions and words. Please." I know she's right. She is my calm before the storm. "Keep your kid away from my family." I open the door and head out front to get Patrick. He is still standing in the corner. I squat down and turn him around. "Patrick, I need you to know you did nothing wrong." I look over my shoulder at Father O'Neil. "I'm sorry, Father, I tried. I guess it's up to you now." MJ takes Patrick's hand, and we head outside.

We get outside and I pull MJ close. "I love you more than you can ever imagine. It will be okay, I promise. I have to go back to work for a bit and then I'm going to go to Andy's house. I'll be home after that." I'm proud of my son for sticking up for his uncle. He has good instincts and knew that it was wrong. MJ gives me a quick kiss and they head home.

Chapter Twenty-Seven

Fitz

When I get to the office, I find Gia by herself. Not what I expected or wanted. "Hey, where is everyone?"

"Sal said until he heard from you, he was sticking close to Kayleigh. She had an appointment out in Roslyn, so he's with her. Can I help you with anything?"

"I'm sorry you were left here by yourself, on your first day, no less."

"Oh, I wasn't totally alone. Travis came by to introduce himself and to check up on me. Lucas O'Brien did the same, and your mom brought me lunch."

"Did we get any actual calls that pertained to work?" I ask. Her eyes grow wide, and she pushes aside her schoolbook until she finds what she was looking for.

"Yes, I'm sorry. Mr. Johnson called. He asked if you can please call him back. He has some information you wanted."

"The next time someone leaves a message like this for me, please text me. I'll be in the conference room if you need me." I'm not mad at her, but I know I came across that way. He picks up on the first ring when I dial him.

"Hey, it's Fitz. What kind of information do you have for me?"

"Always right to the point. I did a little digging on my own and I was able to pull the medical records for Arman Blankenship. The first thing that jumped out at me is he had high blood pressure. He also had a lot of allergies. He was allergic to the sleeping pills he overdosed on. Why would he have them, knowing he was allergic to them? I've found that when most people overdose, it's usually a prescription that they've had on hand. Now don't get all excited, it's not your smoking gun, but it's a good direction for you to look into. I am going to change the cause of death to undetermined, at this time."

"Wow, that's amazing. Thank you for going the extra mile on this."

"No, Fitz, it is me who should thank you. I hate to admit it, but I've become complacent in my job. Thank you, as the saying goes, for holding my feet to the fire. Keep me posted." He hangs up. I'm in shock right now. I'm pissed at myself for not digging deeper into the life of Arman Blankenship. I'm pissed at all the distractions going on around me. I'm about to call Sal and give him a piece of my mind when I hear him come in. I open the door and wave him in.

"What's wrong? You look like someone peed in your cheerios? Did everything go okay with Sergio?"

"I don't want to come off like a dick, but there are too many distractions right now. I've got the situation with your girlfriend. Sergio who was not happy about not getting his money back. We have Gia who should not have been left alone on her first day. I've got a pair of ignorant parents that I nearly lost my shit on today. My kid got punched in the face defending his uncle. The ME called and found something that might prove Arman was murdered, something we should have caught. I've got Andy trying to date again and Stephen sniffing around. Oh, and God only knows if the guy we got on video is a killer. I'm overstressed right now." I run my hands through my hair as I pace around the room.

"Okay, the situation with Kayleigh is under control. She is not staying here. She already leased an office space in Chelsea and put her old one on the market. Lucas came by and I gave him the money, which he took to the charities. Granted, leaving Gia here by herself was not ideal but she is a big girl and it's part of her job. I let Travis know, and he monitored everything from his house. I let Gia know the place is wired, and she was safe. I can't help you with Andy's dating or Stephen sniffing around. Travis sent the photo of the guy with the cap on to a friend of his at Quantico. He should have something back today. As far as the kid stuff, kudos to Patrick for standing up to a bully. Now, are we good here?"

"Now I feel like a prick. I was on overload. I'm sorry."

"No worries. Go home, Fitz, and work on that part of your life. I've got your back." He's right; I need to get out of here and check on my kids.

I head to Andy's house and find him sitting outside while Patrick and Stella are playing stoop ball. As kids, Andy and I spent many hours playing that while MJ always played hopscotch. "Hey, I thought we might talk about stuff. I gather Patrick told you how he got the fat lip."

"No, Mary did, and you know her version was colorful. What is wrong with these people? Do they expect to live and worship in a community of people only like them? I feel bad that our children have to endure all of this when they shouldn't have to. Honestly, Fitz, do you think I should pull Stella out of that school and find a new school and church?"

Right now, my heart breaks for him. He just wants a normal

life like everyone else has. "Andy, think back to when you finally got the balls to tell Mom and Dad you were gay. What I remember most about that was when Dad said to you, 'do you think Fitz and MJ had to come to us and tell us they are straight? No, so you don't have to tell us you're gay.' That, right there, says it all. It is your life to live as you see fit. If this is what makes you happy, so be it. If everyone gave into the pressure of being the same, then this world would never change. Racism would continue. Women would never get ahead. We learn, evolve, and hopefully come out better than before. So no, Stella stays in her school with all her friends, and you stay as an active member of the parish. Don't make me call Mom." He's silent, staring at the ball hitting the stoop. I hope I got through to him. I wish these people could see how kind and caring Andy is. Unfortunately, that type of ignorance will never look past the lies that they believe.

"I can't believe you threatened me with Mom. That's low, even for you."

"Please, how many times have you threatened me with MJ?"

"I decided I'm going to call Stephen tomorrow. Maybe we can get dinner and talk. When we went out last week, I was hurt and closed off. This time, I'll listen with an open mind."

I know he is looking to me for approval, but this is really hard for me. "It's getting late and I'm sure MJ will come out to get us." I swipe the ball and run across the street with everyone chasing me. Finally, some calm in my world.

Chapter Twenty-Eight

Stone

It's amazing to me how some people try so hard to hide their lives, yet they don't realize that nothing can ever be totally erased. Andrew Justice adopted a girl who is the former Vice President's granddaughter. Now, don't that beat all. It took me a while, especially since the adoption was sealed to find out all the information. In this town, it is easier to barter with sex than it is with money. When Arman died, his access to medical records died with him. Which meant I had to find another way to get into someone's medical records. So, I had to perform some extra special sexual favors to get my hands on Andrew's medical records. So not only did Stephen walk out on his sick husband, but he also left him with a kid—a deaf kid to boot. This just confirms my beliefs. The world needs to change, and I'm the one to change it. When I look at my watch, inspiration hits me. If I leave now, I can catch Stephen before he gets home. The subway would be the fastest way to get to midtown. There's also a lot of cameras ever since the world went crazy after Covid. It's nearing rush hour, so they should pack us like a can of sardines and with my cap pulled down low, I think I will be okay.

When I get to my stop, I climb the two flights of steps and pull out my phone. AirTags are an amazing thing. You can track someone without them knowing it. I've slipped them in different items that Stephen carries and last night I slipped one in the pocket of his sport coat while he was in the men's room. I pull up the find my friend app and it shows that he's not that far in front of me. I speed up my pace, knowing I need to reach him before he gets to his building. When I turn the corner, I see him at the newsstand. Perfect. With my hand in my pocket firmly on my Ruger, I slip right behind him.

"Hello, Stephen." He stops abruptly, nearly causing me to slam right into him. He quickly turns around. I slip the gun out of my pocket.

"Stone, what the hell are you doing here?" His voice matching the anger that is clearly written all over his face. Instead of answering him, I push my hand forward. His eyes glance down at the gun I have pointed at him. When he looks up at me, the anger on his face is replaced with fear.

"This is how this is going to play out. We are going up to your place. You will not speak to anyone. When we get upstairs, we will work on your punishment. Now go and remember if you do anything to bring attention to yourself, I will kill everyone around you. You will have to live with the fact that you got them killed." He says nothing as we head into his building. He does his usual wave at the doorman, and we head toward the bank of elevators. It's crowded as we step into one of them and put ourselves in the back corner. "Remember what I said; their deaths will be on you," I whisper. When we get to our floor, there are only two people left. They are too engrossed with their phones to pay us any mind. He unlocks the door, and we head inside.

"See, that wasn't so bad now, was it?" When he turns to say

something, I point my gun at his crotch. "Maybe you want to think twice, Stephen, before you open your mouth."

"Why are you doing this? Can't you just accept that we aren't right for each other and move on?"

"Oh, you mean like you did with Andrew Justice?" All the color suddenly drains from his face. "I see you are surprised, but really, you shouldn't be. You know I wanted more with you. Did you think I wouldn't dig into your past? What kind of disgusting person are you? You left an ill man with a deaf daughter. *Pathetic.* People of his kind, our kind, really shouldn't be allowed to adopt a child."

"Leave Andy out of this. I've moved on, and so has he. It's between you and me now."

I swing my hand so fast that the butt of my gun connects with his cheek. He drops to his knees and curls into a ball. Well, that was easy. To think, he has no idea of what else is coming. "You see, I told you to think twice before you open your mouth, especially since all you do is lie." He grabs the counter and pulls himself up off the floor. His cheek is swollen and bleeding. He sits on the kitchen stool, looking a bit dazed. "I'll ask the questions and then you can speak. Now, what was so wrong with our relationship that you felt the need to push me away? Was it not enough sex, or was it Andrew?" I pass him a towel for his cheek as I head to the bar and pour us each a glass of scotch.

"It was me. It had nothing to do with the sex or Andy."

"Well, if that's the case, then why did you go see him? I mean, if it was over, then it's over."

His face becomes painted with anger. "So that was you. Why were you following me?"

"You knew?" His face gives nothing away and I can't help but wonder what else he knows.

"I wasn't sure, but that entire block—hell—the entire neighborhood, is filled with surveillance cameras."

I pass him a drink before taking a sip, trying to gauge how much is the truth and how much he's embellished. "I have no worries. My face was out of view. However, I'm curious why there is so much security around Andrew. Could it be because of the child? I mean, she is the former Vice President's granddaughter." He takes a sip of his drink but confirms nothing I've said.

"Stone, what do you want from me?"

"I don't know why I'm surprised you even have to ask that. I wanted a long-term relationship. The truth was what I wanted. All I got from you is lies."

"You can't hold me against my will. If you leave now, I will forget all about this."

I finish my drink and realize how disgusted I am by him and his lies, yet I still crave him. "More lies, Stephen. You know it and so do I. Get up and go into the bedroom now. Don't think of trying anything. I have no problem shooting you. You won't be the first, and I'm sure you won't be the last." His eyes grow wide at my confession, but he will never live to tell anyone. I wave the gun towards the bedroom. As he gets up, I grab the bottle of scotch and follow him down the hall. He stops in the middle of the room, his eyes fixated on the bed. When I sit in the chair across from the bed, his eyes finally look right at me. They are a deep green and my cock instantly hardens. We will have to do something about that. "Get undressed." His fists ball at his side, but he doesn't move. "Now, Stephen, resist me and you will only make it harder on yourself." He slowly removes his clothes. There is something about a man in a suit that puts me over the edge almost as much as watching him take off his suit.

"What do you plan on doing to me?"

"Probably the same thing I plan on doing to your precious Andy once I'm done with you." His hands tremble, almost making it difficult for him to unbutton his shirt.

"Andy is my past, Stone. We were over a long time ago. You have nothing to worry about when it comes to him."

“That’s what you say, but your words don’t match up with the emotions you show at the mere mention of his name. Tell me, Stephen, what made him the one? You know, the one you actually married?” I take a swig of the scotch, waiting for his answer. Nothing. “Do you think your silence is going to save him?” Again, nothing. I pull the zip ties and handcuffs out of my pocket. Using the zip ties to clasp his hands together.

“Now that you’ve finally got your clothes off, Stephen, get in the bed.” He climbs into the bed and with his hands clasped together. I then handcuff them above his head to the wrought iron bed. In this position, I can flip him over whenever I want and there is nothing he can do about it.

“Open your mouth, Stephen.” His lips slowly part, and I pour some scotch down his throat. Of course, he’s choking, but he’ll thank me later.

“Now what? Are you going to fuck me into submission?” He chokes.

“Finally, he talks. Oh, make no mistake, I will fuck you every which way I can. You’ll either beg me for more or you’ll plead with me to kill you. Either way, the life you thought you had is now officially over.” I put the gun down along with the scotch on the nightstand and begin to undress. He closes his eyes and turns his head away.

“Look at me!” I grab the lube from the nightstand draw and stroke some on my cock. After all, I’m not a beast, but I’m not about to make it too easy for him. I climb onto the bed and, with a tight grip on his knees, I force his legs apart and spread his ass cheeks. My cock is now perfectly lined up to gain full access to his asshole. If we were making love, it would be different. I would be different, but we aren’t. I’m rough, pushing myself in with no regard for him. He lets out a scream and I punch him in the face. “Shut the fuck up and take it like a man.” I drag my nails deeply down his chest, the deepest at his nipples. When they begin to bleed, I smile and push my cock in harder. His cock is hard. He can't fight the attraction. When he closes his eyes again, I begin punching him in the face. Holding back my urge to come is hard, but I remind myself I'm in control, not Stephen, not my father, not any of the men I've killed. Abruptly I pull out, disgusted with the crying. He curls himself into a ball and continues to cry. I've worked up quite an appetite and decide to go in search of some food. It's not like he's going anywhere.

Stephen

My eyes are almost swollen shut. I've lost all concept of time. My chest is burning but I can't see clearly to see if I'm bleeding. I curl up in a ball trying to wish away what happened. The pain is beyond anything I've ever experienced. I keep thinking back to what Fitz said about the men being killed. I kept my mouth shut because I needed more proof. It's true what they say, careful what you wish for. I am the proof that Fitz needs. When I try to open my eyes, everything is very blurry.

"Stephen, are you ready for round two?"

"Please, Stone, please just leave." His face comes into focus. He is only inches from mine.

"There are those beautiful eyes. Oh, no wait, they are not beautiful anymore because they are all bloodshot." He has a knife in his hand that he waves in front of my face before he presses the cold steel against my cheek. Maybe if I keep my eyes closed, the reality of what's going to happen will go away.

"You can keep your eyes closed for this part. After all, it's not like you'll live to see my handy work, anyway."

I feel the tip of the blade dragging across the skin on my back.

At first, it's painful, but then it goes numb. He pokes the tip of the blade into my skin. Not deep, just enough to torment me.

"You know, when I'm done with you, you'll wish I would have killed you."

"Why did you follow me to Andy's house?" My voice is so raspy, my mouth is so dry that I hardly recognize my voice.

"Stephen, I told you I wasn't following you. The better question is, how did you know?"

"I told you the entire neighborhood is wired up."

"Who told you, Stephen? How did you know it was me?"

I have to protect Andy. "No one told me." He pushes the knife into my left thigh and quickly takes it out.

"Do you see what your lies made me do?" He opens the nightstand draw and pulls out my wedding photo. He puts an X on Andy's face and then grabs a pen and writes next under the X. He uses the knife and stabs the photo to the wall. When he climbs into the bed, he pulls me onto my knees and rams me from behind. He takes one hand and wraps it around my neck like a viper. He is literately squeezing the life out of me. As he pounds into me, he punches my ass, my legs, and my back. Then he switches to my souvenir baseball bat, ramming it into me. I feel like my insides are being ripped apart. I scream for my life, and again he puts his hand around my throat and squeezes. My cries finally grow silent. If this is the end, I hope Andy realizes how much I still love him. I'm sure there's blood everywhere and, eventually, I pass out.

Chapter Twenty-Nine

Andy

After a lot of soul searching last night, I decided to call Stephen. Of course, it went to voice mail. He might not want to talk to me. Maybe he is done. Maybe I waited too long.

MJ took the kids to school today, so I have my morning to myself. As I pour myself another cup of coffee, I remind myself that the answers I need are not at the bottom of this cup. My phone rings and I don't recognize the number. I'm about to let it go to voice mail, but something is telling me to answer it.

"Hello."

"Hi, I'm looking for Andrew Justice?"

"You got him, and you are?"

"Jennifer Probe, I'm a junior partner at The Cooper Alliance Law Group. I really hate to bother you, but my boss Stephen Cooper has you listed as his emergency contact. He is due in court in twenty minutes, and he hasn't shown up. I was supposed to meet him before court today at 8 a.m. to sit second chair. I know I'm rambling, but this is not like him. I don't know what to do."

"He has me listed as his emergency contact. Are you sure? Did you try going to his place?" My hands start to shake so much that I drop my coffee cup into the sink.

"I went to his place, but all the door man can do is ring him to see if he wants me to come up. I mean, what good is that? What if he is hurt?"

"Jennifer, I'm going to get help and I'll be on my way. Can you wait for me?"

"No, I have to be at the court. I'll try to get an emergency continuance, but in the meantime, you need to find him."

This is when my illness really sucks. I can't drive, so I have to rely on others. Fitz will know what to do . . . he always knows what to do. When I call him, it goes right to voice mail. I'm outside now and I see Wanda is still here. I have the keys, not that I would ever dream of driving again. I send him a text.

Me: 911 I'm outside. I need you now.

Fitz comes running out his door half dressed, trying to put his boots on as he runs across the street.

"What the hell, Andy?"

I quickly fill him in on what I know, which is not much really. "Fitz, he kept me as his emergency contact."

"Don't panic. I think Hudson is on the day shift. You call her and tell her what's going on. Have her meet us there to do a well check. The doorman can't stop her from going upstairs."

I call Hudson but it goes right to voice mail, so I leave a message. Fitz is on the phone with the precinct that services Stephen's neighborhood and he asks them to do a well check. He lets him know we are on our way. He passes me my helmet as he speeds into the city. Riding on Wanda is an experience all by itself. Add to that the weaving and speeding, it's definitely not for the faint of heart. We pull up to Stephen's building right as Hudson and her partner get out of their car.

"Hey, Hudson, thanks for getting here so fast."

"Andy, it's okay. Have you heard anything more from Ms. Probe?"

"No. You know him Hudson; this is not like him to just disappear." We head to the front desk. She lets the doorman know what's going on and that we have requested her to do a well check.

"I can assure you, officer, this is a very secure building." He fumbles for the keys on his ring as we head upstairs.

"Protocol says I have to call, which I've done and there is no answer, and then I have to knock a few times and wait to see if anyone answers."

"Sir, on a well check, protocol is out the window. Now open the damn door or I'll kick it in."

He opens the door and steps to the side to let her in. Fitz and I barrel in right behind her. Hudson's partner starts a customary search of the condo. When we reach the master bedroom, I freeze. I've never seen so much blood. It's everywhere. Then I see him, and I gasp. I'm trying to get to him, but Fitz is holding me back. I feel like all the air has left my lungs. Hudson is checking him for any signs of life and calls for a bus forthwith. That's bad. As the son of a cop, I know it's really bad. He is completely naked and covered with blood. Someone carved the word faggot into his back. I want to run to him, take him in my arms and make it better, but Fitz has a death grip on me.

"Andy, he has a pulse. A bus is coming, but I need you to step out of the room and touch nothing. Andy, focus on me, please. The EMTs are here. We need to get out of the way and let them do their job. You can ride with Stephen to the hospital. Come on, Andy, let's stay out of the way and let Hudson process the scene." I hear Fitz telling me all of this, but I can't look away from Stephen. They get the handcuffs off, and they begin working on him. That's when I see our wedding photo on the wall. I squeeze Fitz's arm and whisper. "Look at the wall, Fitz. I'm next." I have no time to show fear, fear for me and fear for my daughter. They are ready to transport him, and I'm racing out the door with them.

"Andy, I'll meet you at the hospital." Is the last thing I hear Fitz say as the elevator doors close.

He's not conscious, but I want him to know I'm here. "Can I hold his hand?"

"Wait until we get him situated in the ambulance." When we get outside, there is a crowd. Typical for New York; everyone needs to be in everyone's business. Finally, we are on our way. I take his hand and hold it tight. "Stephen, I'm here for you. You'll be okay. We will be okay. I promise you." I don't know if he can hear me, but I hope and pray he knows he's not alone.

When we get to Mount Sinai Beth Israel hospital, the EMT's rush him into emergency. The trauma team rushes him away while the triage nurse holds me behind. "Please, I need to be with him. It would be terrible if he woke up, and no one was there."

"What's your name, sir?"

"Andy, Andy Justice." I'm shaking again. It's time for my meds, but I ran out without them.

"Okay, is it okay if I call you Andy?"

"Yes, of course."

"While the doctors are taking care of him, maybe you can help me fill in the blanks. Do you have his insurance information, maybe his wallet with his identification?"

"No, I'm sorry. Everything happened so fast," I say in a panic.

"I'm sure the police are still there. I can call and get the information. Let's finish what you do know, okay?" His voice is very calming.

My phone rings and I see its Fitz. "Hey, Fitz, are you still at Stephen's?"

"Yes, what's going on with him?"

"They are working on him now. Can you find his wallet? They need insurance information." My phone chirps again.

"I took a picture of his insurance card and his driver's license. That should work. Listen, Sal is on his way. You are not to go anywhere without him, do you understand?"

"Fitz, what's going on? Is everyone safe?"

"Lucas is at Mom and Dad's house. MJ and the kids are at Travis's house. Once Sal gets there, everyone will be covered. I just need you to stay put. Do you understand me?"

When Fitz is operating at this level, I know it's bad. "Yes, as long as you have everyone covered. But, Fitz, can Sal stop at the house and get my meds? They are on the counter in the kitchen. When everything happened, I didn't think about anything but finding Stephen."

"I just sent him a text. He stopped at Mom and Dad's, making sure Lucas got there. He'll pick them up. Keep me posted, Andy." Just like that, he's gone.

After I give the nurse Stephen's information, along with my identification, he informs me I am listed as next of kin. I inform him I know he had a living will. I don't understand why he didn't change everything. Next, I place a call to Jennifer to let her know what is going on. Not that I really know much, but at least she knows where Stephen is. As I watch the second hand on the clock tick round and round, I'm reminded that time is a gift that we always wish we had more of, when in reality, we should be thankful for the time we are given. There is a computer screen on the wall that shows each person and the stage they are in their treatment. I watch as Stephen's name travels across the board. Another hour passes and Sal finally shows up with MJ.

"Hey, Andy, sorry I'm late. I wanted to make sure everyone was where they were supposed to be. Your sister wouldn't take no for an answer. Any news, yet?"

"No. The waiting is so difficult." He passes me my pills and a bottle of water. "Thanks for this."

"Fitz said he will get here as soon as he can."

The double doors open, and a nurse comes to get me. "Mr. Justice, the doctor can see you now." With MJ glued to my side, the nurse leads me to a small room with a sofa, two chairs, and two doors. When she closes the door, the silence is eerie.

"Andy, no matter what happens, I'm here for you and Stephen. We will take this one day at a time."

The other door opens and the doctor steps in. He's young, either that, or I'm old.

"Hello, I'm Doctor Wingate, I treated Stephen Cooper."

"Hi, I'm Andy, and this is MJ. How is Stephen?"

"I will not sugarcoat it for you. This was a terrible hate crime. He was forcefully raped many times. He had a lot of rectal damage and not just from the rape. It seems he had been sodomized with some sort of object. He will need plastic surgery to get rid of the carving on his back. His kidney was nicked with a knife. I was able to stop that bleeding. He has a traumatic brain injury from the repeated blows to the head. How severe that is, I won't know until he wakes up. He sustained repeated blows to the eyes. The right eye is worse than the left. His orbital bones are broken around the right eye. The muscle was trapped inside the broken bone. I had to operate on it to get it freed. The knife wound on his thigh was not deep, although it required some stitches. Honestly, I don't know how this man survived all of this. He must have a powerful will to live. He is in recovery now. As soon as he gets into ICU, I will have the nurse come and get you. Do you have questions for me?"

"What can I do for him? How do I help him heal from all of this?"

"We won't know what he will need until he wakes up and we run some tests. Right now, the best thing for him is rest."

"What are his chances?"

"I'll know more when he wakes up."

"Thank you, Dr. Wingate." He leaves and I'm left here totally confused. Not about Stephen's injuries, but why? Why would someone do something so sick and twisted? How did this person get the better of Stephen? But most of all, why am I next?

"MJ, before we go out there, I need to know. How much did Fitz tell you?"

"I never spoke to him. I was at Travis's house helping with the baby when Fitz called him. Travis said Stephen was on the way to the hospital, it was bad, and you were with him. When Sal showed up, I went with him. I would never leave you here alone."

"MJ, our wedding picture had an X over my face and the word next written on it. The picture was stuck to the wall with a knife." Her face pales and she pulls me into her arms.

"We are family, and we will deal with all this together. You need to pull it together and get ready to be by Stephen's side."

The nurse comes in and informs us that Stephen is settled in ICU. We head over and MJ waits outside the room while I go in.

Chapter Thirty

Fitz

Hudson had to wait for her lead detective, Scarpo, to come before she could walk the scene, since she is officially a detective in training. I know Scarpo from one of the FBI training classes for hate crimes I helped Travis with. The delay gave me the time to process everything I was seeing. Everyone has a different way of looking at a crime scene. Some people look at the big picture, some people look at every little detail—I look at both. I usually put in my ear buds to tune out all the noise around me, but I ran out of the house so fast I had no time to grab them. I can't pull my eyes away from the wedding photo with the X over Andy's face and the word *next*. The amount of hate and rage in the bedroom is something I've never seen before. Most killers try to leave nothing of themselves behind, not this guy. Someone trashed the entire condo. He left no stone unturned. When I turn around, I see two Federal Agents walk in that I know. Travis gave me a heads up he was calling the hate crime division. The problem is this: is not a hate crime, it's only made to look like one. I walk up to them and extend my hand. "Hey, my name is Fitz."

"Yes, I'm Chuck Jarvis and this is my partner, Janice Temple. Travis let us know you would be here, and he filled us in on whatever he knew. What else can you tell us?"

"This is not a hate crime. This is the work of a serial killer who started out manipulating gay men to either committing suicide or killing them and making it look like a suicide. His sights were set on Stephen Cooper, who was previously married to Andy Justice. When Stephen tried to reconcile with Andy, it triggered the killer's rage and this is the aftermath. I have some proof, enough that the Medical Examiner changed the cause of death on two of the cases from suicide to cause undetermined. I have a picture of a person of interest that is at Quantico being analyzed. Oh, and I showed Stephen the photo of my person of interest, and I think he recognized him."

"I'm going to play devil's advocate here, so please understand I'm doing my job. Stephen Cooper could be a victim of revenge. How many people has he put away? Maybe that's why he recognized the photo. It's not like he's a tax attorney. I get Andy is family, but I still have to ask, could this be something between them that got out of hand?"

I let what he's saying sink in. I understand he is just doing his job, but he's so far off the mark that it's a total waste of time. "Andy has an alibi. The surveillance put in place by Travis would show Andy coming or going. He can't drive and was home until we came here. As far as Stephen recognizing the photo, knowing him the way I do, I think he wanted to be one-hundred percent sure. He's all about the truth and the facts to back it up." He reaches into his pocket and pulls out his phone and begins typing.

"I like to make notes as I analyze a crime scene. If you wouldn't mind, can you share your notes with me? I can give you my number so you can just forward them to me, and then I'll be out of your hair."

"This is a problem, not for me, but for everyone I've ever worked with. I'm more than happy to share the files with you. However, I don't have any notes to share."

"What do you mean you don't have any notes to share? This is a crime scene. You are supposed to take notes, make a murder book, stuff like that. What do you do if you don't take notes?"

I tap my finger on my temple. The shock registers on his face. "Here me out. I feel if I take notes, then I'm not looking at anything else but the notes. I have to keep looking at things and going through them, so I don't miss a thing. When the case is over, I put everything down on paper as I reflect on the case."

"No murder book, really, not even a board?"

"Sometimes I will make a murder board if I'm trying to have someone see what I see."

"I was told before I came here that you were the best at what you do. A real professional who can get the job done when others can't, and you have no notes?" He shakes his head and goes back to working the scene as if I'm not even here. I pass Janice my business card.

"If he wants the files, he can call me."

I turn and walk out. I need to be with Andy. That's my place right now. I try calling Sal and it goes right to voice mail. I hop on Wanda and head to the hospital. Rush hour is over, and the traffic is moving at a good clip. When I walk into the emergency room, I find Sal in the waiting area.

"Why aren't you with Andy?!"

"Before you lose your shit, MJ is with him. She wasn't taking no for an answer. She said her brother needed her, and this was where she was supposed to be. I can't control her. Hell, for that matter, you can't control her. I would have gone back, but Stephen is in ICU. Andy is with him and MJ is standing outside the door looking through the window."

"If she ever did what I told her to do, I would probably drop dead of a heart attack. What about my parents and the kids?"

"Travis has the kids, and Lucas is with your parents. Your mom even canceled Bingo for tonight."

"That can only mean one thing: she is scared. What's the status on Stephen?" He rocks back and forth on his heels, takes a deep breath, and slowly exhales. "I know it's bad, Sal."

"MJ said he has a long road of recovery ahead of him, if he makes it."

"I've got to get back there. I can't leave all of this on MJ to handle." When the doors open, I am going to fight my way in. MJ is standing there with a look of such despair. A look that makes it hard for me to breathe. She's not moving and the tears, my God I can't take the tears. I rush to her and pull her into my arms. She is trembling as she wraps her arms around my waist and holds on tight.

"He coded, Fitz. They were able to bring him back, but it doesn't look good. Andy had to be sedated. They are putting him in a room now. I've never seen my brother fall to pieces, not even when he found out he has Parkinson's. Fitz, he told me about the photo. I'm scared. I can't lose him—any of them. You need to do what you do best and fix this." I scoop her up and carry her to a chair in the waiting room. She's in my arms and I rock her. I hear a commotion and when I look up, my mom and dad are coming into the hospital. My mom is at the desk with her holy water from the Vatican and her rosary beads, demanding to see her son-in-law. My father is trying to slip the security guard money, while Lucas is trying to explain to the guard that it's not a bribe. This is my family, folks.

"Sal, can you please do something with them?" I move the hair from MJ's face and wipe the tears. "Hey, the rest of the family is here. I need you to take care of Mom and Dad. I have to get back to Andy. You know, if anyone can get through to him, it's me." My mom sees us and rushes over. She makes the sign of the cross with holy water on our foreheads. "Mom, please stop. Just pray to God for healing. I need to see Andy." I put MJ in the chair and head to the nurses' station. After I explain everything to her, she let me know Stephen is still alive and Andy made them aware of his Parkinson's before they gave him anything. She agrees to take me to Andy's room.

They sedated him and put him in a room not too far away from Stephen. Seeing Andy like this breaks my heart. He saved me when I was six and now it's up to me to do the same. I pull the only chair in the room closer to the bed. When I take a tight grip on his hand, he stirs but doesn't wake up. "Andy, if you can hear me, Stephen is still alive. You know I'll always tell you the truth." At the mention of Stephen's name, Andy's grip gets tighter. "Dear God, I need your help tonight. I'm sure you know what's going on here, and you don't have time to listen to the long version of what happened. So, I'm going to flat out beg you the help Stephen. No one should go through what he did. Love is love. Andy is hurting, too. Please do what you know is right. Thank you, Amen." After being buried alive, I feel like I have a closer connection. My phone chirps, letting me know I have a text message.

Janice: We found a mini baseball bat souvenir under the bed. We believed he used this to beat and sodomize Stephen. I also called the hospital and let them know.

Me: Thank you. Have you found anything else that might help to identify him?

Janice: Not yet, but there is a lot of evidence here to process. It seems he also took a shower to clean up. There were a lot of prints, but the best set was on the empty bottle of scotch. I will keep you posted. The security footage showed the guy coming in with Stephen. It also shows when the guy left. As requested, we sent it to Travis for further analysis.

Me: Thank you.

A baseball bat. A shiver runs up my spin at the thought of what Stephen went through. Andy stirs again and opens his eyes. "Hey, Stephen is still alive. That's good news. He's fighting hard and will need you to pull yourself together and be there for him."

"Always so blunt. What time is it?"

"Around three a.m. Oh, and Mom and Dad are here." He closes his eyes and for a moment I thought he went out again.

"She probably brought the holy water, right? I need to get back to Stephen."

He tries to move, but he's still feeling the tail end of whatever they gave him. "Let me get a wheelchair. The last thing we need is you falling. You rest while I talk to the nurse." He closes his eyes and I go in search of a wheelchair. I find nurse Debbie, who gets a wheelchair and helps me get Andy into it. I thank her and we head back to ICU to check on Stephen. When we get there, the staff lets me go in with Andy. No wonder Andy lost his shit earlier. Stephen looks worse than when I found him.

"Fitz, why did someone do this to him? Is he coming for me? What about Stella? Are we all in danger? I mean, look what our kids are facing in catholic school every day. I've dealt with homophobic people all my life, but nothing like this. What do we do? How can we be safe?"

"As to why this happened, I won't have that answer until I find out who did this. I promise you; he will never get that close to you. Stella, along with Patrick and Mary, are all staying with Travis, so they are safe. I promise you, Andy, I will find out who did this. As far as what's going on with the kids at school, we stand up to these people. They are ignorant bullies, who think their way is the only way. The one thing we will not do is run and hide. Someone has to break the chain or this shit will never end."

"But why does it have to be us? Look at the price Stephen is paying."

"We will be here, and we will support him every step of the way. I'm going to give you some time alone with him. I need to check on the family." I lean in and whisper in Stephen's ear, "You need to fight because this is far from over."

Chapter Thirty-One

Stone

The judge was not happy that I called in sick today, but it took a lot longer to wash all that blood off of me than I thought. I've never created such carnage and suffering like I did at Stephen's place. Usually, I assist them along the way to their final destination—hell. hell. Let's face it, these people sure aren't going to heaven and, for that matter, neither am I. Maybe we will all get together when I get there? I wonder how long it took for Stephen to die. I'm sure someone from his firm has found him by now. He was supposed to be in court at 9 a.m. Surely there will be something on the local news. I keep flipping through the channels, but there is nothing. Maybe it's in *The Post*. Stephen hated *The Post*. He always called it a gossip-filled rag. All the more reason to love it. I pull it up online but there is nothing. Maybe he didn't die, although, I really gave it my all. Maybe it took longer because I really didn't want to give him up. After all, he is the first one I really wanted to keep.

Before I leave this earth, I need to find out what made Andrew

Justice, a man with a chronic illness and a deaf child, better than me. I've kept a journal on every man except Stephen. I thought he was different. Sadly, he was not. It's my way of remembering them after they are gone. I'm staring at the blank page, wondering where to begin. Maybe the day he was appearing before Hon. Justin Cunningham. Oh, I've seen him around the courthouse many times, but that's really the first time I officially met him. His dimples were front and center in my face during the entire trial. Even the judge made mention to me how good looking he is, or should I say was? I scroll through the photos on my phone, looking for just the right one. He would never let me take his picture and he never wanted to take a picture together. That, right there, should have been a sign. I find my favorite one. He's smiling in his sleep. That's the only way I could get a picture. I wish it was me he was dreaming about. However, I'm realistic enough to know it's not me, but I'm pretty sure it's his precious Andrew.

I know I left a lot of evidence behind. I couldn't help it. I snapped when I realized he was willing to die for Andrew. Well, I guess there is no time like the present to find out. It looks like I'm going to be spending more time in Brooklyn. Thanks to Stephen, I know there are extra cameras in that area. I grab my lucky hat, take one last look around, double checking that all of my traps I set for uninvited guest are engaged and head out. Maybe I could pay a condolence call, or maybe it's too soon.

Fitz

So far, Stephen made it through the night. Of course, Andy never left his side. The doctors are a little more optimistic, but he still has a very long road ahead of him. Everyone will ask him what he will do. I don't have to ask him. I know Andy. He's never stopped loving

Stephen even though he broke his heart, that's Andy. I'm sure he will take care of Stephen until he can't take care of himself. Lucas took MJ to Andy's house, and she packed some clothes along with his medication. Mom and Dad will not leave until they see Stephen. I learned a long time ago when it comes to Mom and Dad, they are very stubborn, so I pick and choose my battles wisely. Sal is back at the office keeping everything running. Travis has all the kids on lock-down. While I'm waiting on the results from the crime scene, I head to see Father. O'Neil.

The first thing I do is head into the church and light a candle for Stephen. After that, I find Father. O'Neil in his office, battling that printer again.

"Good news, Father, Sal found an extra printer in one of our storage closets. He's going to come by this week and set it up for you." He stops what he is doing and gives me the biggest smile. Now I have to order a printer and have Sal bring our old one here. So technically, it is an extra one. Splitting hairs, but it works.

"Your mom called me to tell me about Stephen. How bad is it?"

"The doctor said if he made it through the night, then his chance at surviving this increases. I got to tell you, it's really bad. You know I've seen a lot in my lifetime . . . stuff I wish I could unsee, and this is one of them. He is going to need a lot of surgeries down the road. Plus, the emotional wounds of what he went through might never heal."

"I know this is too soon to ask, but do you think this could bring them back together?"

"You are such a hopeless romantic. Only time will tell. I want to bring you up to speed in the Arman Blankenship case. The medical examiner changed the cause of death as undetermined. He also did the same for Justin Michaels. We proved that Franklin James was, in fact, a suicide. I think the guy that assaulted Stephen could be the guy behind all of these crimes. I have a picture and a video clip to show you. Let me know if you've ever seen him." First, I show him the video, then I pass him the photo. He stares at it, running his thumb over the picture, and then closes his eyes. Finally, he opens his eyes and passes me the photo.

"So many people pass through these doors. Some stay and become part of the family, like you did. Others are just passing through, not sure what they are looking for in life. Honestly, I don't know, but now that you showed me everything, I will pay closer attention."

"That's really all I can ask for. Now, what should I do about the kids? What was said was very hurtful. The parents are just as bad as the son. I tried talking with them, but that only made it worse."

"They have decided to move out of the parish. You know, Fitz, I really tried to get through to them. I asked them to get to know Andy before they pass judgment. They want no part of it. I told them I would pray that God softens their hearts. People like that will come in and out of our lives. We can only do our best. Besides, you've got bigger problems . . . Mary Elizabeth. She is a combination of you and MJ. She is going to give you more gray hair than you can imagine. I will pray for you." He laughs and puts his hand on my shoulder. At least I have him in my corner.

"Thank you. I'll send Sal over with the printer. I'll keep you up to date on everything."

I head out and make my way over to the office. If this guy was here the other day, maybe he went into one of the businesses. This is a close-knit community of all different nationalities. We don't see the differences between the people here. As I make my way up 5th Avenue I stop in random stores, but no one recognizes him. Before I know it, I'm at the office. Gia is at her desk totally into something on her computer. When she sees me come in, she smiles.

"Hey, I thought that maybe this guy took the subway. If I could look at the camera footage from that day and we can find which station he went into, maybe we can pull all the Metro cards. I called

Travis, and he got me into the camera system for the city. That man is amazing. How is Stephen? I don't know him, but I stopped by my church before work today and lit a candle for him."

"I'm sorry, Gia. I haven't had my coffee, yet," is the only answer I can give to her multiple questions. She gets up from her desk and gets me a cup of coffee, along with a pastry.

"My mom made the pastry, and I brought in the coffee pot. I don't know how you people function in here without one."

"Your mother made these? I think I'm in love." She laughs and shakes her head.

"Don't get too excited. I mean, my parents own the bakery, and we live upstairs. These were the first ones that were ready, so I grabbed some for the office."

"Did you have to burst my bubble?"

"Keeping it real, boss man."

"Any luck with the photo?" I take a seat at my desk, which is next to hers, and lean in to see her screen.

"Maybe if I went a little wider with the subway stops. Look at this and tell me what you think? It's from the 77th Street station. I got it from the camera at the bodega on the corner. It caught this guy wearing the same hat. Now I know there could be a million guys wearing the same hat. The guy he is talking to doesn't cover his face." She tilts the screen so I can see better.

"Holy, Gia, that's it! You are amazing! Print that out for me, please and thank you."

"Okay, not sure what I did, but I'll take amazing."

While she does that, I get Travis on the line. "I'm at the office and you are on speaker. Gia is here. You need to get into Andy's dating app. Remember, I told you about the date that Andy was going on, well it was a set-up."

"Fitz, slow down and tell me exactly what happened."

"Gia found the guy with the hat outside the bodega at the 77th

Street station. He is talking to a guy for maybe a few minutes. He clearly gives him money and then the guy disappears as he goes down into the subway station. The guy that the man with the hat met is the same man that Andy met for coffee. It was a fucking setup, and I let Andy walk right into it." In one fell swoop, everything from my desk is now on the floor. Gia runs out of the conference room with the print-out in her hand. She looks at the stuff on the floor but says nothing.

"Fitz, calm down. I need to know which app it is."

"I'm trying to remember, but I wasn't focused on that as much as the people he was looking at. Wait, I ran his date's picture through Sal's facial recognition program. It would still be in the memory, right?" Gia is back at her computer and quickly pulls it up.

"Travis, I got it. His name is Jason Basile, but when I pull up the Metro cards with the right time stamp, there is no Jason Basile. There is a Jason Anderson, so Basile is probably fake."

"Thank you, Gia. Fitz, she's right. Basile is an alias that shows up clean. Anderson has many arrests for prostitution. That's why Sal's program said he was clean. I'm texting you his address now."

"Gia, text Sal the address and tell him to meet me there, but wait for me before he goes in." When I look at the address, a bad feeling comes over me. Ozone Park Queens; right near Sergio's club.

Chapter Thirty-Two

Andy

MJ BROUGHT ME ENOUGH MEDICATION AND CLOTHES FOR a week. While the nurses are doing their usual vitals check, I step into the bathroom to get cleaned up. The man in the mirror is staring back at me, and it is frightening. I wasn't the one who went through everything that Stephen did, but it's wrecked me just the same. I told him I wasn't his difference, but maybe he was trying to show me in other ways. The one thing this has made me realize is that I still love him. Did he hurt me? Hell yeah. I was so broken that it took me a couple of years to finally feel like I was healing. Maybe we were supposed to work on this together, work on finding our way back to each other. Why did it take something horrible like this to make me want to open my heart again? So many questions and so few answers. When I step out of the bathroom, there is one nurse still in the room. She is talking away and at first, I think she's talking to me, but I realize she is talking to Stephen.

That's when I see his eyes are slightly open. I let out a yelp, and he slowly turns his head toward me.

"Don't go scaring our boy now that he just woke up. I paged the doctor to let him know, and he is on his way."

I step closer to the bed so he can see me better. His eyes are very swollen, but they are a little open. He opens his mouth to speak, but he can't. He closes his eyes, and a tear runs down his cheek. I take his hand, knowing that the connection, our connection, will always be strong. "Stephen, you will be okay. I'm here and not going anywhere. You need to fight to live, and I will fight for us." I lean in and place a gentle kiss on his forehead. Doctor Wingate comes in, so I back away to give him some room.

"Hello Stephen, I know it hurts to open your eyes. I just want to take a quick look. You are lucky they got you here so quickly. I have no doubt that saved your life. I'm going to keep you sedated; we need to give your body time to heal. In a few days, we can talk about what's next for your treatment. You can have ice chips, if you need them. For now, just rest. Andy, let's step outside."

"Okay, so what don't you want him to know?"

"He's only just waking up and I don't want to overload him with all the measures we took to save him. He doesn't know that he has a temporary colostomy bag. I will reverse it in six months, depending upon how he heals. He will need more surgeries, but right now it's all about resting. His body is still fighting to survive. The emotional end of this will kick in once he is more lucid. He's got a very long road ahead of him. The best advice I can give you is to keep him calm and don't treat him any differently because of all he's been through. I'll be back to check on him before I leave."

"Thank you. You've done so much for him . . . for us."

"It's going to be okay. Now get back in there. A familiar face is the best medicine."

I head back into the room and he's out again. He was my rock when I was first diagnosed with Parkinson's and now, I need to be the rock for him. When I take his hand again, he stirs for a moment and squeezes it.

"Tell Fitz it's Stone." His voice is gravely. I have no idea what he means, but he's out again. I grab my phone from the tray table and call Fitz. It goes right to voice mail. For some reason, I feel like this is important. I call MJ.

"Is everything okay?"

"Calm down, yes. Stephen woke up for a minute. I also had a consultation with the doctor. He is healing and needs rest. He came to again and said, tell Fitz it's Stone. I have no idea what he's talking about, and Fitz's phone is going right to voice mail. I think it's important, MJ. Get in touch with him, please."

"On It. Hang in there."

"Stephen, if you can hear me, I passed along the message. Now rest."

Waiting, lately, it seems like that's all I do.

Fitz

Sal sees me pull up behind his car and gets out of his car. My phone chirps with a text from MJ.

> **MJ:** Stephen woke up for a minute and said to tell you it was Stone.
>
> **Me:** Okay, I'll call you later.

I show Sal the message and put my phone away. "Do you know who Stone is? Could it be the guy in the hat?"

"Fitz, if it was important enough for that to be the first thing Stephen said, then yeah, it's probably him. Gia brought me up to speed on why we are here. However, this neighborhood is run by Sergio Puccio's crew. What are the odds?"

"Like, what are the odds that your girlfriend just happened to be friends with one of the victims in our case?" A deep frown creases his forehead.

"You can't be right, Fitz. I mean how could she be involved?"

"I'm not doubting she was friends with Franklin. However, I think she knew about the money, but she couldn't find it. The same way Sergio's goons couldn't find it. I mean, let's face it, it was a fluke I found it. She had his computer and was probably trying to figure out the password. What did you tell her you did for a living?"

"Partners in an investigation firm."

"And . . ."

"She asked if I was a cop. I said, no, I'm a computer geek. Shit."

"When she realized you got right into Franklin's computer, she hightailed it out of there. Granted, we did find her where she said she would be, but that doesn't mean she didn't make a phone call along the way."

"Do you think the attack on Stephen was part of this?"

"No, I really think Stephen picked the wrong guy to get involved with. Either way, we need to find these two bastards. I think we should start with the apartment house on the corner." I hit all the buzzers until someone lets us in. We knock on the fifth door. I hear someone moving around, but they don't answer. "Pizza Delivery." I shout out so whomever is in there can hear me.

"I didn't order a pizza." It's a guy's voice.

"Well, I can't bring it back, so it's free." The guy opens the door a crack and Sal pushes it in so hard the guy is on his ass, looking up at us.

"On your feet, bright star." Sal lifts him up with one hand while I make my way around the apartment, checking if anyone else is here.

"Clear." I yell out to Sal. He drags him by the throat into the living room and throws him onto the couch. I pull the picture out and shove it in his face.

"Who's the guy with the hat?"

"Stone, I don't know his last name. He only goes by Stone."

"Why did you meet with Andrew Justice for coffee?"

"That's what this is about? Stone paid me a C-Note to meet the guy and see what he was like. It was easy money for only fifteen minutes of my life, so why not?"

"Where can I find Stone?"

"I'm not his keeper. Try his work."

"Okay, where does he work?"

"I know he works for the criminal court in the city. He clerks for some judge. I think he wants to be a lawyer. That's it, everything I know. Are we done?"

I'm already out the door with Sal right behind me. When we get out to the street, I stop at Sal's car. "Do you have your laptop with you?"

"Yeah, what are you thinking?"

"If he works for the court, his fingerprints have to be on file. Do you have access to IAFIS on your laptop?"

"No, but Travis has direct access to it, since he is still a consultant with the FBI. I'll text him the information. In the meantime, we could head towards the court. If we go back through Brooklyn instead of going through Queens, we can avoid a lot of construction."

"I'll meet you at the courthouse. Tell Travis to try and find out his last name." I'm about to head out when Sal's phone rings.

"Travis, what do you have for us?"

"His name is Stone Carver. He clerks for Judge Cunningham. He's not at work today, so going to the court is a waste of time. I have a home address for him. It seems he rents a studio on Dutch Street, just off of Fulton Street. Apartment 5C. I'll text you the address. Now that we have a name, I'm going to see what else I can find on him. Fitz, I have Lucas still staying at the hospital with your parents."

I hit mute on Sal's phone. "Are you going to ask him, or am I?"

He glares at me as he unmutes the phone. "Travis, can you please see what you can dig up on Kayleigh Barrett? I'll explain it all later. We will text you from Stone's apartment." He hits end and the directions pop up.

"You can be pissed at me all you want, Sal. If the shoe was on the other foot, I would expect you to do the same. I'll meet you at the apartment." I pray when we get there it will end peacefully, but I have my doubts.

Chapter Thirty-Three

Fitz

The first thing we do when we get there is look at all the outs he could have. There are a lot of buildings in Manhattan that have more than one entrance or exit. Sure enough, his building has two. "I think we should call Travis before we head in and see what he found out." Sal quickly agrees.

"Hey, we are here. There are two ways in and out of the building. Did you find out anything else?"

"Yeah, do not go in! I repeat, do not go in! I got a call from Chuck Jarvis from hate crimes. They figured out it was Stone Carver from the fingerprints he left on the scotch bottle. They are on their way to you with the bomb squad. Apparently, Stone was issued an Administrative Separation from the army. Fitz, he's a trained explosive expert. They want to evacuate the area first."

"Damn it, that could take forever. Maybe I could at least go up to the fifth floor and have a look around. Sal will wait downstairs for Chuck." I don't wait for an answer. When I run inside, I notice there is no one around in the lobby, so that's a good thing. The elevator is making its descend and when the doors open there is only one person inside. A man with a baseball hat and blonde hair sticking out the sides. I'm blocking the entrance as I usually do; a bad habit, I know. He looks up, smiles, and says, "excuse me, this is my stop." Instead of stepping aside to let him out, I pull my piece and push him backwards hard. He stumbles backwards and grabs onto the railing. The doors close and the elevator starts to move up, which means someone has called for the elevator. I reach over to the panel and hit the emergency stop button. This causes the elevator to abruptly stop between floors. The elevator system automatically cuts power to the motor and hits the brakes so there is no free fall. I learned all this one sweltering summer when Andy and I worked maintenance for an elevator company.

"Hello, Stone. Where are you off to in such a hurry?"

"Who are you, and how do you know my name?" His face pales as his eyes never leave sight of my gun.

"You messed with my family, and now I'm going to be the one to put an end to you. You left a very messy scene in Stephen's home. Did you think you would get away with what you did to him? Did you really think you would get anywhere near Andy? What about the others, Arman and Justin?"

"Did you see, Stephen? Even if he lives, he will never be the same. His precious Andy will only have the broken shell of a man. Come to think of it, not really a man at all." His words dripping with hatred.

I want to shoot him. It takes all of me not to take aim and blow his fucking face off. However, there are cameras in here and I don't know what's in his apartment. "Stone, today is your lucky day. As much as I want to blow your face off, I will not stoop to your level. The courts will take care of you. I can put you at every one of those suicides. I'll give the families what they need most—closure ."

"There is just one problem with your plan. I rigged my entire apartment with enough C-4 to take this entire building down. I have a deadman switch that I built into one app on my phone. If I don't enter the numbers in the correct sequence . . . boom!" He's got a grin on his face that I'm itching to wipe off.

I would love to think that he's bluffing, but I know better. He is a man that has nothing to lose. I hit the call button and Sal's voice comes booming over the speaker.

"Fitz, are you okay?"

"I have Stone with me. He said his apartment is wired with C-4 and he has a deadman switch on his phone. Is the bomb squad on scene, yet?" Before he can answer, the elevator begins to move. The doors open and there are at least fifteen men with rifles drawn. I holster my gun and leave them to take care of this mess.

"Fitz, what the hell were you thinking? I told you we wait for the bomb squad."

"Well, I wasn't expecting the doors to open and Stone to be standing there. I'm heading over to the hospital to let them know the worst of this is over."

"Okay, I'll stay here and finish up."

I take off and leave him to deal with the aftermath.

Andy

Stephen has been coming in and out of it all day. He stays lucid a little longer each time. Every time he sees me, he smiles and then cries. I don't know the hell he went through; I only know the aftermath that he is dealing with. It amazed the doctors that he's alive and how much progress he is making in a short amount of time. Doctor Wingate said when Stephen completely wakes up, he might not remember much of what happened. He said when trauma is that bad, the brain can block it out as a means of self-preservation. All I know is we might not be together, but I never stopped loving him. There is a light tap on the door and when I look up, Hudson is here. I wave her in.

"Hey, I know it's only one person at a time, but they saw the badge and let me in. The nurse said he is healing. We are all praying for him, Andy."

"Thank you so much for everything you did to get us in to his place as quick as you did. I can never thank you enough."

"Andy, we are all family, and we go the extra mile, no matter what. MJ went home to take care of the kids. She said she will be back later with some food for you. Your parents have been here since we brought Stephen in yesterday. I decided with the nurse to bring them in for five minutes and then I'm taking them home. Is that okay with you?"

I get up and give her a big hug. "Of course, it's okay. Thank you for taking care of my parents. I know they can be a handful." When I turn around, Mom is wheeling Dad through the door. She waits for no one. The first thing she does is pull the bottle of holy water out of her pocketbook. She sprinkles some on me and some on Stephen. After which, she does the sign of the cross on both our foreheads. She then takes out her special rosary beads from the Vatican and starts praying. Dad waves her off and pushes his wheelchair closer to the bed. He takes Stephen's hand and after a minute, leans in as close as he can get.

"Son, you better fight hard because when this is over, I have a bone to pick with you. Come on Annie, Hudson is taking us home. She can't wait around all day for you."

Hudson tries not to laugh as she gets them out of the room. When I check my watch, I realize it's been hours since I gave Fitz the information from Stephen. I just want this nightmare to be over for all of us.

I wish I could climb in bed next to him and hold him close, just like he did when I told him I had Parkinson's. Since I can't, I do the next best thing. I pull my chair as close as I can and try to rest my head on his shoulder. "I'm here, Stephen, always."

Chapter Thirty-Four

Fitz

It's been a long crazy week, and it's far from over. I miss what I consider normal family time. Andy's life has been turned upside down. I always knew that he still loved Stephen, but it was hard for him to see that through the pain of rejection. I don't know what is going to happen with them, but I know Andy will take care of him until his dying day. That's Andy. When I get to the hospital, I see MJ waiting for the elevator.

"Hey, beautiful, I miss you." I wrap my arm around her waist and pull her close as I nuzzle that tender spot just behind her ear. The elevator door opens, and we step inside.

"MJ, there is no one in here. Want to have a quickie?" She almost drops the food she's carrying.

"Fitz, you don't do quickies." She pulls my t-shirt free of my jeans and one hand is raking her nails over my abs and the other is balancing the food. Gifted.

"Oh, babe, I would so try doing it right now." Then the elevator door opens, she turns and walks out. Two nurses walk in. My shirt is half off, my cock is hard, and all I can do is smile as I race after MJ.

When we get to Stephen's room, he's not there. I instantly panic. I mean, I know what the man went through. The nurse informs us they moved him to a private room. They felt he was doing much better, and they needed the bed in ICU. We find his room. At least it's quiet.

"Fitz, I'm glad you came. What happened with that information I gave you?"

"Andy, you and Fitz can talk about everything after you eat."

"There is nothing to talk about. We got the guy. The details don't matter right now. The only thing that matters is Stephen." With that, Stephen opens his eyes the best that he can. I reach into my coat pocket and pull out my Ray-Bans. I put them on Stephen. "I think you need these more than I do right now."

"Did I hear right? You got him?"

"Yeah, while I was out playing cops and robbers."

"Touché, Fitz." He smiles, and then he's out of it again.

"MJ, are the kids okay? What did you tell them?"

"I kept them home from school but made sure I got the work they missed. Travis is doing it with them. They know nothing about Stephen, so I told them that a friend of yours was very sick and you went to help him. You can explain it better when you get home."

"Fitz, what are we going to do about the Di'Mazza family?"

"Andy, I handled it. Everything is being done, so all you have to think about is helping Stephen."

"What exactly do you mean by 'you handled it?'"

"They decided to move out of the parish, and no, I had nothing to do with their decision. It's getting late, we are going to head home. Are you going to be okay here?"

"Yes, the chair is a recliner, and the nurses brought me blankets and a pillow."

MJ and I head out after reaffirming to Andy and Stephen that

Stone has been captured. The nightmare is over. However, I still have loose ends to tie up. Starting with the bomb and the deadman switch. When we get to her car, all I want to do is go home with her and make love all night long.

"Hey Fitz, what's wrong?"

"A lot to still do and a lot of unanswered questions."

"I'll meet you at home and we can have some quiet time tonight." I lean in the car window and give her a kiss. She waves as she drives away, and I'm reminded of how blessed I really am. My phone vibrates with a new text message.

Sal: It's done. Everything has been disarmed and Stone is on his way to county lock-up. Meet me at the office.

Me: On my way.

Traffic is light; I make it back to the office in twenty minutes. I'm glad to be done with Stone, but I have a bad feeling that I can't shake. When I get to the office, Sal is already there. "Hey, what happened when you finally got into Stone's apartment?"

"He wasn't kidding about the C-4. He had stockpiles of it. The federal government is going to impose federal charges for the bombs and the hate crime. He is probably going to claim insanity. Right now, he is in the holding cell at the federal court house. What's bugging you, Fitz?"

"Who's to say he doesn't have friends that will get him out, or better yet, what if he makes bail?"

"Even though we know what he did, he still has rights. You realize that Stephen will most likely have to testify. Do you think he will be able to?"

"When I think about Stephen, the tough as nails lawyer, I say *hell yeah*, however, I also saw what was done to him. It's not just the physical stuff, it's everything. The fear is real for him. Can he ever experience intimacy again? Will he ever let himself be loved or love another? You know it's like Andy with his Parkinson's. He's always afraid to tell anyone he has it. He feels he is judged by what he can't do, like not driving. Usually, the kids end up taking the keys away from one of their parents. That's expected as someone ages, but Sal, I was the one who had to tell Andy he can't drive anymore. It was hard on both of us, especially since cars were his life. He still holds his Master Mechanic certificate with pride and, I'm sure, sadness, too."

"I didn't realize you were the one to do that. That must have been very difficult."

"I gave him a spare key to Wanda. I told him if it was a dire emergency, do what you have to do. It showed him I still trust him, even with Wanda." I get up and make a cup of coffee. I think I like this one cup pot Gia brought in. I think I like the pastries even more.

"Travis sent over everything he found on Kayleigh. She has no ties to Sergio. I think she was friends with Franklin and maybe he confided in her. I don't think we will ever know. Once she saw Sergio's goons coming around, I think that scared her enough to tell me. Either way, no one but the charities got the money. Sergio has his ledger back and the thumb drive is locked away."

"What about you? Are you going to continue having a relationship with her?" I'm keeping my fingers crossed he sends her packing.

"No, I feel like she used me and, after that, I lost all respect for her."

"I agree, but if you decide to use a dating app, please think twice. I don't think I can handle another case like this again. Oh, I have something I need you to do for me. Before you say anything, humor me. I ordered a printer, and they will deliver it tomorrow. I need you to take the printer and put it in our storage room. Then I need you to take it out of the room and bring it to Father. O'Neil." I don't get a chance to explain. He is laughing so hard, he is practically in tears.

"You told Father. O'Neil you had an extra one in storage, didn't you? Oh, Fitz, you really keep things interesting. I will keep your secret. It's getting late. I'm going to head out and you need to get home to your family. I'll see you in the morning."

He leaves and I start to close up when I get a text from Janice.

Janice: FYI Stone was being transferred to New York-Presbyterian Hospital for a psychiatric evaluation when he escaped. We are still piecing it together, but we think he had inside help. We requested security be beefed up at the hospital that Stephen is in. I will let you know when I find out anything else.

That bad feeling that I couldn't shake just reared its ugly head. I try calling MJ, but it goes right to voicemail. I need to update Sal and find out where MJ is.

Quickly, I dial Sal before he gets too far away. "Miss me already?"

"Stone escaped. I need you to go to the hospital and keep an eye out for him. I'll be there soon." I hang up and call Travis.

"Stone escaped, where is MJ and the kids?"

"They are all here, safe and sound."

"Good. Keep it that way. I'm on my way to the hospital. I also sent Sal there, too. When I can, I'll check in.

The guy is unhinged, and I wouldn't be surprised if he went after Andy and made Stephen watch. Wanda is the fastest way to get there, so I don't waste time. I hate to make this phone call, but I'm left with no choice. I call Andy and it goes to voicemail. The hair on the back of my neck is standing up, and I know he is in trouble.

Andy

The doctor started Stephen on clear liquids. I was helping him eat some broth when Stephen's face turned pale. "What's wrong? Do you want me to get you something else? Should I call the doctor?"

"Go ahead and tell your precious Andrew what's wrong."

I swing around so fast that I drop the broth on the floor. "Who are you, and what do you want?" I have a good idea I know who he is, but I'm trying to stall.

"Stone, leave us alone." Stephen's voice is so raspy it's almost hard to understand him.

"I don't think so. You know I've had a terrible day, Stephen, and it's all because of you. I was arrested and sent to jail. Do you know how humiliating that is? Especially, since I've been friends with the guards for years. When they learned what I was accused of, they looked at me like I was some sort of leper. Then they put me in leg irons, a straight jacket and tried to take me to a psychiatric ward. You and I both know there is nothing wrong with me. I was doing what was best for everyone, including you. Lucky for me, I have a lot of friends in high places."

He waves a gun around. I step in front of Stephen to give him some sort of protection. I don't know what good that does. Stephen tries to reach the call button, but Stone points the gun right at my head as he grips my arm so tight, I nearly drop to my knees.

"Stephen, touch the call button and I blow Andrew's brains out. That would leave his daughter without a father." He knows about Stella?! Stephen puts his hands up to show him he's not touching anything.

"What do you want? You want to kill me, then you just kill me, but leave Andy out of this."

"No, that would be too easy. That would make you happy. I'm not happy, so why should you be? I'm going to have some fun with your precious Andrew and figure out why you want him and not me. After that, I'm going to do to him what I did to you. Doesn't that sound like fun?"

I hear a lot of commotion outside the room. I can only hope Fitz has figured out I'm in trouble. Now some sort of alarm goes off. "You will never get out of here alive," I inform him.

"You are not helping your cause. That just makes me want to shoot you." He presses the barrel of the gun to the side of my head. I begin to shake.

"If you keep shaking, I'm going to shoot you before I even get to have some fun with you."

The door to the room opens, and Fitz comes in with his gun aimed at Stone's head. "He can't stop shaking on your command. I knew I should have blown your fucking face off when I had the chance."

Sal steps into the room behind Fitz with a gun pointed at Stone. I look at Fitz and his eyes are almost black. When he is this focused, I know it can't be good for Stone. Maybe I can defuse the situation before someone ends up hurt or, God forbid, dead. "You are quickly becoming out numbered. Why don't you put the gun down?" That didn't help. If anything, it made it worse as his grip on me gets tighter.

"Well, Andrew, if that's the case, then I really have nothing to lose . . . do I?"

The sound is so loud and there is blood all over my face. I feel my knees start to buckle beneath me as the weight of Stone's body brings me down. Fitz moves at lightning speed and pulls me away from Stone.

"Andy, it's over. It's not your blood. Let me help you get cleaned up." He pulls me into the bathroom while the room becomes flooded with police and the medical staff.

"It's really over, but why did he do all of this? I don't even know him." He wrings out the washcloth and tries to get the blood off of me, but it's everywhere.

"I can only surmise he seemed to be very jealous or what Stephen had with you, what he still has—your love. You need to face the fact that beyond the rejection is a man that still loves you. As to why Stone did what he did to the other people, I don't think we will ever know the truth."

"Fitz, why does this shit keep happening to us?" His eyes darken with the pain he carries with him.

"Andy, we don't live in a bubble. As long as there are bad people in the world, I will always fight my hardest to right the wrongs and protect the innocent. That's who I am, who we are."

I let his words sink in and I feel my adrenaline rush easing. We head back into the room to face a barrage of questions before we can truly say it's over.

Chapter Thirty-Five

Andy

It's been three months since Stephen was attacked. The outside wounds are healing, but it's the emotional wounds that I'm most worried about. The attack has changed him, hell, it's changed all of us. He has been getting counseling, but today, for the first time, he has asked me to attend a session with him. I'm happy, yet nervous. It's never easy to put yourself out there for someone else to pick apart, especially, since we have so much unsaid stuff between us. The ride to the hospital is long. MJ wanted to drive me every day, but the alone time in the Uber gives me time to think. This too will be changing since he will be moving to a rehab facility, which he wants no part of. When I get to his room, I find him dressed and waiting for me.

"Good morning. You look great, how are you feeling?"

"I'm fine, Andy. The doctor came by this morning and informed me that I will be transferred to a rehab facility in Brooklyn. This might be a good time to tell me what's going on."

"I was hoping I would be here before the doctor. I arranged to have you in a facility closer to my house. While I'm putting it all out there, you might as well know I had your place cleaned and it's going on the market."

"So, now you are making life changing decisions for me? I love that you are helping me, Andy. Especially, when I was such a prick toward you. However, you should have told me first."

"Maybe this is something we can talk about with your therapist?" My tactful way of deflecting doesn't work on him. He looks at me and, for a quick second, I can see there is a world of hurt he is hiding.

"Andy, I was going to talk to you about this in the therapy session today, but I guess now is as good a time as any. I love you and nothing will ever change that. I want you in my life but not like this. I've been pieced back together on the outside like Humpty Dumpty, but I don't know if I'll ever be the man I was ever again. I think it's best if you to go back to your life and leave me to figure mine out."

So much is racing through my head right now I think it might explode. I let him leave me once and I did nothing about it. I'm not going down that same path again. I get up and close the door, since what I have to say is no one's business but ours. I turn around and he's trying to make his way toward me. "I let you go once without a fight and that is never going to happen again. You can either let what happened to you define who you are going forward, or you can fight to get to a better place than you are now. The Stephen I know is a fighter, a man who does not subscribe to pity parties. The choice is yours, however, what you don't have a say in is my love for you. You can't tell me when to stop loving you and why. That's on me, babe, all on me. I can and will lay down the ground rules. I have a daughter to protect. I will let you into her life, but understand this, Stephen, right here and right now; if you ever hurt her or treat her in any way that is no respectful, I will cut you out of our lives so fast, and there will be no going back." He takes a step toward the door, and I step in front of him, blocking his exit. "You might want to have a seat, Stephen, I'm far from done." He slowly walks to the chair and gingerly sits down. I shake my head at the thought this man thinks he doesn't need any help.

"Are we going to our therapy session?"

"Not just yet, I need to have my say. You left me high and dry, cold as ice and never looked back. I know I should have come to you so we could talk about Stella, but everything happened so fast, there was no time to think. Honestly, you were the last person I thought would not back me up. I really thought we were solid, able to fight any storm, I was wrong. I know that now and for that, I'm sorry. But I still wouldn't have changed a thing. You are going into a rehab facility near the house. You will not fight me on that one. I can't say that we will ever be *us* again but I'm willing to leave that door open. As far as my daughter, when I feel that we are in a good place, I would like for you to meet her, but it will be on my terms. There will be many bumps in the road, but I'm prepared to ride them out with you. Are you okay with all of this?" He looks up at me and a tear slides down his cheek. I want to pull him into my arms and reassure him he will be okay, we will be okay, but I can't, not yet.

"Why do you love me so unconditionally? Andy, I'm damaged goods, at best. Why would you want me in your life after all I put you through?"

I drop to my knees in front of him and gasp both his hands in mine. "The heart wants what the heart wants and no matter how hard we try, it will always win. I love you, Stephen, and you are not damaged goods. You are a man who suffered a great deal at the hands of a lunatic. None of what happened was your fault. If you give into the pain and humiliation he inflicted, then Stone wins. I need you to fight with all you've got. Fight for you and fight for us." I get up and pull him into my arms. He holds on tight and begins to cry gut-wrenching sobs. I'm not shaking and I'm not crying. I'm totally supporting him. After a bit, he pulls back and wipes the tears from his face.

"Andy, you would have made a great trial lawyer."

"Who knows what the future holds for us." There is a tap on the door before it opens and the nurse is there with a wheelchair. She informs us it's time for the therapy session. We head out and, for the first time in a long time, I can see the light at the end of the tunnel.

Epilogue

Fitz

When you are busy, it seems time moves so quickly, but when you're not, it leaves you with too much time to think. Shooting Stone saved, at least, Andy's life, but it's never easy when you take a life. Besides going to my meetings, I've found myself spending more time with Father. O'Neil. He lets me putter around the church doing little odd jobs even though I have a job of my own. Sometimes it's just a welcome break from all the bad in the world.

One of the best decisions was hiring Gia Milano. Not only is she a great worker, but her parents own a great bakery that we benefit from. She has taken to calling me boss man all the time and I'm okay with that. She is one of the few people who can anticipate what I need before I even ask her.

Andy moved Stephen to a rehab facility that is close to our neighborhood. At first, I was worried that Andy would spend all his time nursing him back to health, but he has found a balance. He had the colostomy reversed. He had reconstructive surgery on his cheek and last week he had his last skin graph on his back to erase the carving. Now he can work on healing the inside. I speak from experience when I say that will be a much longer journey than he thinks. Today, Andy is going to bring Stella after school to meet Stephen. I know I should trust that Andy would do nothing to upset Stella, and I do, but I will be there, too. One perk of being a godparent is having a say in raising a child.

When I get outside, Andy and Stella are waiting for me. "Are you sure you don't want me to drive us there?"

"No, the best conversations happen when we take our time not rushing to get someplace."

"Have you and Stephen talked about where he will go when they discharge him?"

"Always direct and to the point. Well, he sold his condo, which I can't blame him. I wouldn't go back there, so he is moving into your old apartment at Mom and Dad's house."

I stop dead in my tracks, with my mouth hanging wide open. "What the hell? What about Hudson?"

"You see, Fitz, the family left it up to me to tell you. They all know how crazy you can get. She's grown up and leaving the nest."

"Where the hell is she going? You better tell me everything."

"Okay, she got her permanent assignment, which she knew you would flip out about. She's going to the Bronx, more specifically Arthur Avenue. I knew she would speak with Dad about it and she wanted to live in the neighborhood she would work in, plus travel time is a bear. She feels she is finally ready to head out on her own."

"Dad was okay with all of this?"

"He trusts her and he knows she is great at her job. He told her the door will always be open for her and he had no problem throwing Stephen to the curb if he needed to. I think he is still very mad at him. Mom is happy Stephen is moving in because it gives her someone else to mother."

"How do you feel about Stephen living there?"

"It gives us space and, honestly, Fitz, I'm not ready and I don't know if I will ever be. When I met him that night at Peter Luger's, I told him flat out that I'm not his difference. I tried to explain it, but he never really got it. I want to be the first thing he thinks about and the last thing he thinks about. He needs to put my feelings first. These past months, he's watched me take care of him and he said he finally gets it. So, we will take it one day at a time."

"Andy, I hope you know what an amazing person you really are." I scoop Stella up in my arms and we head inside. When we get to his room, we find him dressed in sweats, sitting in a chair. I put her down and stay in the background. I notice he as an ASL handbook at his bedside. So, at least he is trying, but it doesn't mean he is ready for a family. He may never be ready, but I'm sure Andy will deal with that if it happens.

Stella is trying to sign slowly so Stephen will learn. She also lets him know her grandpa is teaching her to read lips. When Andy tells her where Stephen will live, she tells him all about her grandma's chocolate chip cookies. I know they will be okay, so I give a quick wave and leave, giving them the family time they are creating.

I decide it's time for me to head back to work . . . my actual work not the putzing around I've been doing at the church. Walking the Avenue brings back so many memories, but even with the coming and going of so many people, it still feels like home.

When I get to the office, I find Gia in the conference room with someone while Sal is on the phone trying not to raise his voice. He gives up and slams the phone down.

"Okay, what's the problem?"

"That woman in with Gia is a potential new client. I was trying to confirm some of the information she gave me, but I keep hitting that brick wall."

"Why don't you take a deep breath and tell me why she is here?"

"She thinks she married a murder, and she wants our help to prove it."

My ass lands in the chair next to his desk and I'm looking at him like he is telling a really bad joke. "You are not serious, are you?"

"Yes, very serious."

"Well, what makes her think that?"

"She has only been married five months, and she started getting cryptic notes left on her car and at the gym."

"That doesn't make him a murderer." He tosses me some photos, some rather *disturbing* photos.

"Those were with the notes. At first, she thought it was a prank, but then this morning she found this tucked under the windshield wiper blade of her car."

He holds up a bloody knife in a plastic bag and I feel a chill run up my spin. I get up and head into the conference room, with Sal following close behind me. Gia gets up and introduces us.

"Fitz, this is Lindsey Bridges. I'm sure Sal filled you in on her case."

"Hello, Lindsey. I understand you think you need our help. Why don't you start from the beginning for me."

"It all started on a dating app."

"Really, a dating app? Which one might I ask?" Her hands are shaking as she passes me her phone. I don't bother to look at it, instead I pass it to Sal with a smirk on my face. Everyone knows the way I feel about apps.

"It was all good, but then it all wasn't. When all this stuff started showing up, I decided to look deeper into his background. There are a lot of holes, big ones in his timeline."

"What does Rodger do for a living?"

"He's a long-haul truck driver."

"That could account for the holes in his timeline. You can't jump to any conclusions."

"I thought the same thing until I compared police blotters from where he said he was and the crimes that took place."

Since true crime shows and podcasts have taken off, everyone thinks they are the next Nancy Grace. She opens her bag and pulls out newspaper clippings. I glance through them and realize she might be on to something. "Okay, Lindsey, we will take your case. Now let's get started."

The End, for now.

Coming Soon:
Bloody Matrimony
A Fitz Series book 5

Other Books

The Unraveled Trilogy

The Unraveling of Raven

Darkness Into Dawn

Shattered Lies

The Bench

Unraveled: The Next Generation

The Letter: Dear Michael

Hard To Love

The O'Hanlon Family Trilogy: Social Rejects Syndicate

Ciarán: Book One

Patrick: Book Two

Ronan: Book Three

Coming Soon!

Discrete Investigations

The Fitz Series

Uniquely Mine, Book One

Silent Innocence, Book Two

It Will Always Be Us, Book Three

I'm Not Your Difference, Book Four

Standalone Books

Maribel's Decadent Miniatures

The Heist

The Christmas Contest

Out of the Shadows

About the Author

Theresa Sederholt was born and raised in Brooklyn New York. She is a graduate of Campbell University in North Carolina, with a degree in Criminal Justice. Theresa now calls Florida home, with her husband, a professional chef, and her two dogs.

Experiencing life first hand is what she does best. Believing she can do anything has put her in many crazy situations. Whether it's babysitting a pig farm or cutting the top off of a mini truck; nothing is ever out of reach. Her list is endless, A to Z.

Theresa's beliefs are pretty simple. There isn't a luggage rack on the hearse, and give a girl Nutella and espresso and she can change the world.

Theresa enjoys connecting with her fans. She can always be reached through her website at:

www.theresasederholt.com

Made in the USA
Columbia, SC
21 June 2025

59641830R00124